Hiding Behind The Couch Series

Chain of Secrets

by
Debbie McGowan

Beaten Track
www.beatentrackpublishing.com

Chain of Secrets

Published 2016 by Beaten Track Publishing
Copyright © 2016–2023 Debbie McGowan

Paperback ISBN: 978 1 78645 328 0
eBook ISBN: 978 1 78645 025 8

Cover Design: Debbie McGowan
Licensed stock images:
usage is not indicative of the models'
identity, activities or preferences.

Love Hearts and Swizzels
are trademarks of Swizzels Matlow Ltd.
www.swizzels-matlow.com

Beaten Track Publishing,
Burscough. Lancashire.
www.beatentrackpublishing.com

Contents

Pray for Love

Fast like short lasting flower petals
That in love will start to crumble and smash together
Thirsty for a forgotten dark whirlpool
Oh god others beg for happiness and peace
But me I will remember in my heart. And hold,
Yesterday like a tussock

I will close my sad soul like gold in a chest,
And make it a temple of love.
My soul does not pray for happiness, past joy, or
The belief she asked from me
Upon this terrible day, like a ship wreck,
It needs to be saved

Without help you're withering fast
Like a poppy in ripe grain and flax
Oh god I'm not praying for happiness, joy, or relishment

I'm afraid this pain won't die;
Like the holy ignited fire inside of me
But suddenly it dies and becomes ash
Although overnight I fear it will ignite again into passion

'Pray For Love', by Desanka Maksimović
English translation by Nebojsa
http://2ndcupoftea.com/2014/04/02/time-padlocks-bridging-gap-
romance-history

Prologue:
The Viaduct of Love

IN THE THREE-A.M. darkness of an insomniac night, the boats moored along the canal bank transformed into shapeless black monsters, slumbering so lightly that the slightest disturbance set their multiple eyes restlessly flickering. No noise with the still waters and the absent breeze; Josh took firm steps into the silence, punctuating it with the squelch of his soles upon the rain-wet towpath and the too-fast pounding of his heart. He reminded himself that only he could hear it and squeezed his fist tighter around the metal object in his pocket. It had absorbed his heat, and its presence, lost to the absence of sensation in his palms, was evident only in the recollection of how cold it had been when he had first taken it from his memory box.

Onwards he went, glancing up briefly to check his progress towards the viaduct before returning his gaze to the glistening ground beneath his feet. A light flutter of wings echoed through the early morning, a duck startled; Josh held his breath until the peace returned but kept moving. Twenty years had passed since he last traversed the towpath, yet it appeared largely unchanged. The mooring bollards sported a new coat of paint; the gravel was more evenly spread with no deep potholes, although he avoided the puddles in case they were deceiving him. A few more streetlights spilled their amber payloads over the viaduct, picking out the small ripples carried from the sluice gates a quarter of a mile beyond the bridge.

Some things were different, of course. He had only ever visited in daylight, except for that one time when, lost, they had cycled up and down country lanes for what seemed like hours, eventually coming across the canal some twelve miles east of their hometown. They had followed the towpath all the way back, passing under the viaduct as dusk fell; it was night by the time they were safely home. But even at dusk, it had been less formidable.

And this morning, as it had been for his visit twenty years ago, he was alone.

Reaching the viaduct, the loneliness multiplied, becoming as numerous and unquantifiable as the feeble surface ripples yet still singular in its ambition. Josh slowed to a halt and examined the concrete slope that ascended from the towpath at an incline— he had estimated often—of thirty degrees. As children, they had scrabbled with ease, on hands and knees, as close to the top as they could get and still lie with their backs pressed to the cool concrete, a shady haven on a hot summer's day.

At seventeen, when Josh had first visited alone, the slope had proved no more difficult than on his previous encounters. Indeed, it had been far easier than those occasions when they had discovered winter was not the ideal time to climb the ice-slicked surface. In winter, their sanctuary became a bitter grey wasteland, rejecting rather than welcoming. Thus, their cycling routes developed a seasonal flavour, and they knew to avoid the canal if they ventured out at all during the colder months.

Spring was Josh's favourite time of year and not just for cycling. He loved the long, bright days, the fresh air, fragrant with blossom, the sights, scents and sounds of newborn flora and fauna, although he was quite certain his adoration of the latter was not something he had naturally acquired. In childhood, he had not wished for a puppy or a kitten or any of the other pets his classmates pined for, not even after the death of Claude, his grandma's ancient cat.

One of the biggest wonders of friendship for Josh had been realising that it took no effort to show interest in what was important to his friends, for those things likewise became important to him. Before he knew George, Josh's understanding came from the death of his parents, and he had considered life and death as two distinct, sudden states: being and not being. George's wisdom, coupled with Josh's own observations, had helped him to understand the delicate balance, and nowhere was it more apparent than in the seasons of spring and autumn. Had he been an artist, the rich, varied colours of early autumn would have inspired him to pick up a brush, but he was not, and all too soon the trees were fully bare again.

The passing of the seasons. Thirty-seven he had now witnessed, through the windows of classrooms and lecture halls, his surgery and his office. The ten years in childhood and adolescence that they had been everywhere together were long, long gone. Now it was summer again, and while the humid heat was not the only reason sleep eluded him, he was grateful for the cover of night. Josh's pale complexion did not do well in the sun, which also turned his hair from the colour of sand to that of lightly whipped cream.

The summer after his twenty-first birthday, he had faced a far greater obstacle than hot weather or ice or the ordinary darkness of night, and he had considered coming here one last time. Either way, it would have been to say goodbye, but he had made a promise, so he had stayed away until he was sure he could keep it.

Hidden from the world yet always visible to him, he wore the constant reminder of that promise twice over, and in time, he had adapted to the loss of feeling in his hands. He could use a can opener, a pencil sharpener—even scissors were not the adversaries they had once been. He was self-sufficient, which was good reason to be cheerful. He had achieved independence— financially, practically, emotionally—but for this one small indulgence and the hope that resided within.

Now tinged deepest pink from dawn edging into the day, the slope, Josh could see, was mostly dry, but his soles were not, and he half leaned, half sat with feet upturned, resting his heels on the ground. Glancing over his left shoulder, he saw the dark outline, not yet discernible from the shadow of the road above.

A car passed overhead. *Progress.* He had returned expecting the worst, but not once since they had made it 'their' viaduct had it been fortified or repaired. Nor, it would seem, had any others laid claim to this place, and he was optimistic his secret had remained undiscovered.

Josh slid his heels a few inches upwards, taking care not to touch the wet ground as he turned to his side, rolling and slowly drawing his legs up until he was on his hands and knees, ready to begin his climb. The distance he needed to cover was no more than fifteen feet, yet the exertion of climbing such a steep incline stirred up the broth of emotions that was a permanent feature in his life. It required his constant attention to stop it from boiling over, and visiting the viaduct threatened to be the thing that blew the lid off the pot.

The light now was more than adequate for him to clearly see his target. Even to him it looked like nothing more than a rusted metal ring, but he knew it was there, obscured from view by the uneven settlement of the structure that had created a two-inch sill above the concrete wedge and below the road. As he neared it, he reached out and curled his fingers over the jagged lip, noting a little more settlement, though still not quite enough grip for leverage.

Ducking his head, Josh crawled up and along to the right, searching with his fingertips, listening for the tinkle of steel on steel that would confirm no-one had found it. The sound came, and he sighed in relief. He lifted the chain free and wiped the dust and cobwebs from the heavy brass padlock, his fingertips unable to discern the engraving, though the trace memory was intact.

Most Ljubavi: The Bridge of Love. Josh's grandma had told him a story about the bridge over the Vrnjačka River in Serbia where young women wrote their names, along with the names of their beloveds, on padlocks that they then attached to the bridge. There was more to the story, he recalled, of a young woman whose fiancé had proposed to her on that very bridge and then left her, and the padlocks were the hopes of other women that their fate would not be as hers.

Hope. It was all he had. He slid the second padlock from his pocket and turned it, the face reflecting the pink-orange glow of the sky, casting their initials in shadowed relief.

JS – GM

With a short twist of the key, the lock sprang open; Josh looped it through the next free link in the chain, clicked the lock shut, tugged it to check it was secure, and returned the key to his pocket. With the chain still in his hand, he rolled onto his back and held it close to his chest, allowing his memories to coalesce, knowing that once he returned the locks to their hiding place, he would leave those memories with them.

Many times on the walk home he fished out the key again—not easy when it was so small and flat that his numb fingers could not feel it. Each time, he panicked that he had dropped it, and he checked again and again. To distract from obsessive thoughts, he forced his mind back to the Bridge of Love. It was truly romantic, and he had once found a photograph in a library book, discovering that it was more a walkway over a stream than a bridge over a river. Nonetheless, it was a beautiful story, and he couldn't help but think his solo re-enactment fell far short. A modern concrete viaduct over a canal was neither beautiful nor romantic; indeed, there were many more delightful bridges—with stunning arches and rich, ancient brickwork—not much further away. But not one of those bridges was *theirs*.

Back at home, Josh went straight upstairs and propped the ladder against the wall, clinging as he climbed, cursing his fear of heights and that he must face it alone. With one hand firmly gripping the top rung, he stretched to unlock the loft hatch and reached a few inches inside, locating and lifting down the small case in which he kept the objects most precious to him: meaningful trinkets, his childhood diaries…the key.

At Vrnjačka, he recalled, the keys had been thrown into the river so that no other could breach the bonds between the lovers. He marvelled at the notion that love could be so simple, or perhaps those women were fortunate; if not fortunate, then naïve. For even after all these years of unconditional friendship, he could not make sense of nor understand what he was supposed to do with George's admission. A further twelve years had passed since he had made it, but the truth of it had not dwindled.

I think I love you.

Josh opened the case and looked down at the photo of the two of them, taken when he'd received his Master's degree. He touched a fingertip to George's smile.

"I think I love you too," he whispered. He dropped the key into the case, closed the lid, and shut it away.

Josh
(aged 10)

Dear Diary,

It's the last day of junior school, and I'm trying not to be sad. Everybody else is happy about it, but that's only because it means the summer holidays start tomorrow.

The other fourth years don't seem to understand. In six weeks, we'll all be the smallest children in a big new school, which will be hard. When our new headmaster came in to talk to us, he said that even the big children would get lost because it's a new school for everyone.

I'm not scared. I've been the youngest person in my class since infants, and sometimes it was annoying when the new children started in September and they kept asking, "Why are you small?" Now I'm taller than some of the girls, the others don't notice me like they used to, and my class have forgotten about my mum and dad.

Well, mostly they forgot by themselves, except for some of the boys, and George 'helped them to forget'.

WHAT YOU DOING?"

Josh quickly shut his diary, blushed brightest pink and kept his head down. If he didn't make eye contact, the other children usually left him alone. But not this time.

Shaunna, who was in his class and the only pupil he'd ever talked to besides George, turned her head to the side and squinted. "Is that your autograph book?"

"Y-yes," Josh lied.

Shaunna reached into her cardigan pocket and, with a bit of an effort, tugged a small lilac notebook free. She held it out to Josh. "You sign mine, and I'll sign yours."

Josh flicked his eyes up to her face. She was smiling, not teasing. "I…erm…" He frowned and tried to think quickly.

"It's OK if you don't want to."

"No. It's…" He sighed and rubbed his head, playing for time. He could tell she wasn't going to take no for an answer unless he told her the truth, and he didn't want to do that. His classmates already thought he was strange, and in a way, he supposed they were right. They played football in the park, went to Cubs or Brownies and got grounded for being late home. He read books, wrote stories and only left the house to come to school or to play out with George.

He didn't want Shaunna to think he was strange. She was one of the few he liked because she was kind and clever, and her long, red hair fascinated him. He wanted to plait it and unplait it and watch it swish over her shoulders like a rippling stream of flames. *Best not to tell her that.*

He had an idea. Turning his diary upside down, Josh rose to his feet and held the cover open so that Shaunna could only see the blank back page.

"I get to be first!" she said excitedly and scrawled in rainbow pencil:

To Josh,

You are the cleverest boy I have ever met. Don't forget about me when you sell your first invention and make a million pounds.

Love Shaunna H xxx

"I like your pencil," Josh said, holding the page close to his face so he could study the way the colours intertwined through each letter.

"Thanks!" Shaunna said. "Your turn."

Securing his diary between his thighs, he took Shaunna's autograph book and flicked through to the first blank page. It was almost at the end of the book.

"You have a lot of friends."

"I have a lot of autographs, but I only have two *real* friends."

Josh wrote:

To Shaunna—

"Do you want to know who they are?"

"Hold on a minute. I'm thinking what to write."

"OK." Shaunna stood quietly and watched.

To Shaunna,

Thank you for being kind to me after my dad died.
You—

"Can I tell you yet?" She bounced up and down on the spot.

"Do you need the toilet?"

"No. I want to tell you who my two friends are. It's good." She nodded to emphasise how good it was.

Josh narrowed his eyes and made a prediction in his head before he asked the question. "Who are your two friends?"

"Adele, which you know, because we always sit together and stuff. And the other one is you."

"Me?" He blinked in surprise. He'd thought she was going to say Adele and one of the other girls in their class.

"Yes, you," she confirmed.

"But..." He frowned. "Why?"

"Because you were kind to me when my grandma died, and you read stories to me, even though I got fed up and kept asking you questions. I know George is your best friend, and I'm not jealous. It's good he's your best friend, like Adele is my best friend. Sometimes she can be really annoying, though. You're not annoying. When the others say you're a snob, I say, 'No he's not. He's shy.' Because you are shy, aren't you?"

"Erm, yes, but—"

"I knew it. You should try football, you know. It's fun. And George plays it." She pointed across the playground, to where George and the rest of the fourth-year boys were enjoying their last game of football in primary school. She turned back to Josh. "Have you finished yet?"

He shook his head and returned to his writing.

To Shaunna,

Thank you for being kind to me after my dad died. You have the most beautiful hair in the world. It is like liquid fire, and you shouldn't tie it up. Thank you for being my friend. Now I have two friends too.

Love from Josh x

He handed the book back to Shaunna, and she read what he had written. Her forehead creased, and she smiled the tiniest smile. "I forgot your dad died. I mean, I didn't because you don't forget things like that, but it isn't always in my head."

"I understand," Josh said. He stayed quiet and waited for Shaunna to read the rest. She turned pink, and then giggled, and then gave Josh a huge, beaming smile.

"Don't you want people to sign your book?" she asked.

Josh shook his head.

"Why not?"

"Erm, well…"

What he was about to do was a tremendous step for him, but he wasn't sure what else he had to offer. Because that was what friends did: they played together, and they were kind to each other, and they trusted one another. "Can I tell you a secret?" he asked.

"Only if you want to."

"I do."

"OK then." She took his hand and tugged, until they were both sitting, cross-legged, on the hard stone playground.

"This isn't my autograph book," Josh admitted.

"What is it?"

"It's my diary."

"Oh." Shaunna picked up a white stone and doodled on the ground: solitaire noughts and crosses. "Sorry."

"It's OK. I'm glad you wrote in it. I'm going to keep it forever. Do you have a diary?"

"Yeah, but sometimes I can't be bothered to fill it in."

"I write in mine every day."

Shaunna looked at Josh in awe. He shrugged. "That's hard work!" she said.

"Not really. I like doing it. I've got four diaries now."

"Four? You've been keeping a diary since you were—" she counted back on her fingers "—six?"

Josh nodded. "After my dad died, Mr. O'Malley told me to. Every time I went to see him, he asked me how I was feeling, if I'd been thinking about my mum and dad, and I said I couldn't remember, which was true. So he said whenever I thought about them, I should write it down, and then we could talk about it. It was silly."

"I don't like Mr. O'Malley," Shaunna said. "Adele does reading and writing with him, and he gives her lots of homework. Did he give you homework?"

"I suppose keeping a diary was my homework."

"Except now you do it because you want to?"

"Yes. But I don't write about my mum and dad anymore. I write about the things that happen during the day. Like before, I was writing about it being our last day." Josh studied the diary's cover, smoothing his hand over the black fabric. It wasn't a 'real' diary; it was a notebook with lined pages, and he had to write the date at the top of the page, which was good. Some days, he didn't have much to write; on other days, he filled several pages.

Writing it down, it felt like he was locking all of his thoughts and feelings away, hundreds of tiny secrets he dared not share with anyone else. Not that anyone else would be interested, he thought, but when he listened to the other children, it was as if they saw the world in a completely different way—even George, who *did* think Josh was strange, but that was OK. George said his strangeness was why they were best friends. The thought made Josh realise something.

"Why aren't you playing with Adele today?"

"She broke friends with me."

"What for?"

"I'm going on holiday tomorrow, and she wanted to come, but my mum said no. We're going to visit my aunty in Ireland."

"Do you and Adele usually go on holiday together?"

"Never ever. But her mum and dad fight all the time, and she wants to run away. I promised to send her a postcard, and I'll go round and play when I get back. I hope she doesn't run away. I hope we make friends again."

"I'm sure you will," Josh said sincerely. Before George came to their school, Josh didn't have *any* friends, and he knew how lonely it was.

Shaunna nodded and gave him a smile. "Yeah, we will." She got up and brushed down her skirt. "How come you and George don't play together in school?"

"We do sometimes. But we like doing different things. He likes playing football. I hate it. I like reading. He thinks it's boring."

"Are you best friends in the holidays?"

"Yes. We do lots of things together in the holidays. If the weather's dry, we go out on bike rides."

"Sounds like fun!"

"It is," Josh agreed. That was what they had done last summer, and he was very excited about it. George had grown too big for his old bike, and he'd got a new one for Christmas—or new to him. Josh could tell it was second-hand, but he didn't say anything to George about it. He thought George and his mum were probably a bit poor, as George had school meals, and even though he was only eleven, he had a job, sort of, helping one of the older boys who lived near him to deliver the free paper.

Josh didn't mind spending his money on George. If he didn't do it, then he wouldn't have a friend to play with or, at least, they'd have to stay in all the time, and George would get bored. They couldn't even go to George's house, as his mum worked all day. But hopefully the weather would be nice this summer; Josh had bought a map and was finding places they could cycle to within a ten-mile radius of their hometown. So far, he had fourteen different places on his list, and his grandma had bought him a set of panniers to put their packed lunches in.

The bell sounded the end of lunchtime, and Josh and Shaunna joined the queue along with the rest of their class, although the boys took a little longer to make it across the playground, still kicking the ball between them as they jogged over.

"Pick it up, please," Mrs. Kinkade shouted from her classroom window. Dan—who was captain of the football team and also in their year—picked up the ball, and he and George joined the queue behind Josh and Shaunna.

"Did you score?" Josh asked.

"A couple of times," George answered.

"*Five* times," Dan boasted on George's behalf and then ran past them, pushing in at the front of the queue.

"I hate him," Shaunna hissed and angrily folded her arms. Josh frowned and opened his mouth to ask why, but George nudged him in the side to shut him up. Josh closed his mouth again.

Soon they were back inside, and all that was left of their last day was their leavers' assembly, followed by their class party. The fourth years were asked to come out to the front, and everyone in their class was awarded a certificate and a book voucher. The younger children clapped loudly, and Josh remembered sitting where they were, watching the out-going fourth years. It had felt like forever before they would be standing at the front of the school hall for the final time.

Back in their classroom, their teacher let Shaunna sit at Josh and George's desk for their party, which wasn't really a party. All of the children had brought in sweets and snacks, and the teacher had brought lemonade and a big cake wishing them 'Good Luck'. The sweets George had brought were all stuck together, and he spent ages trying to prise them apart with his ruler. It didn't work. When he went to the boys' toilets to wash his hands, Josh took the opportunity to ask Shaunna a question that had been on his mind since lunchtime.

"Has anyone ever read your diary?"

"No."

Josh considered her answer for a few minutes before saying anything further. "Mr. O'Malley used to read mine, but it's different now, and I don't want anyone to read it. I keep it hidden away, but what if someone discovered it?"

Shaunna shrugged. "Why don't you get a diary with a lock?"

"It's not a real diary. It's a notebook. And I have four."

"So ask your grandma if she's got an old vanity case or something like that with a lock."

Josh knew there were lots of old hat boxes and cases in the attic. Maybe his grandma would let him use one of those. "That's a good idea," he said. "Thank you."

George came back from washing his hands and got waylaid by Dan, who asked him if he wanted to play football in the park in the summer holidays. George and Dan weren't really friends, they just played football together, but Josh was worried by Dan's question. If George was busy playing football, what would happen to their bike rides?

George didn't make it back to their desk before the bell sounded for home time, and Josh and Shaunna left together. As they walked across the playground, Josh pointed to the parents waiting at the gate.

"Is that your mum?" he asked, his gaze fixed on the woman with long red hair like Shaunna's, although it wasn't in plaits. It lifted in the summer breeze, the sun reflecting off the shiny curls.

"Yeah," Shaunna confirmed airily. "Will we still be friends in high school?"

"I hope so." Josh wondered why she thought they might not be. It was only six weeks away.

Shaunna held out her hand with her fingers in a fist, except for the little one. Josh's tummy suddenly felt funny. He'd seen the other children do it, but no-one had ever done it to him. Though he was nervous, he lifted his hand and hooked his little finger with Shaunna's, staying quiet while she made the vow.

> *"Make friends, make friends,*
> *Never ever break friends.*
> *If you do, I'll flush you down the loo,*
> *And that will be the end of you."*

She released him and grinned. "That's it now. We're friends forever. Have a good summer, Josh." She skipped away to her mum.

"You too," he called after her.

"Josh!"

At the sound of his name, he spun on his toes and waited for George to catch him up.

"You walking home?"

"Yes."

"OK. What's the matter with your face?"

Josh touched his cheek and shrugged.

"You've gone really pink."

"Sunburn?" Josh speculated, knowing full well it was nothing to do with the sun. He was still blushing from the friendship ritual.

"Bye, Josh!" Shaunna called as he and George passed by. Josh smiled quickly and kept his head down. George started giggling.

"Shush," Josh whispered.

"Why? Do you fancy Shaunna?"

"No."

"Are you sure?"

"Yes! Why did you nudge me at lunchtime?"

"Did I?"

"When she said she hated Dan."

"Oh, yeah. Because Dan won't let her play footy."

"Because she's a girl?"

"Yep. She's amazing at football."

"Amazing," Josh repeated. "Are you sure *you* don't fancy her?" Now both of them were giggling. "Plus, Dan is Adele's boyfriend," Josh added.

"What's that got to do with anything?"

"Why Shaunna hates him, I mean."

"Oh. So, like, she's jealous?"

"I don't know." Josh peered sideways at George and watched him for a while. He was frowning, deep in thought. "You like him?"

"Dan?" George asked. Josh nodded. "We're not even friends really."

They continued to walk, both in thoughtful silence, until they reached the road where Josh lived. George paused at Josh's gate. He was still frowning.

"What's the matter?" Josh asked.

"I don't think I'm ever going to have a boyfriend. It's too complicated."

"It probably gets easier when you're older."

George looked at him doubtfully.

"When you're a teenager, not a grown-up," Josh clarified.

"Who cares?" George shrugged. "Do you want my book voucher?"

"Don't you want it?"

"I want you to have it." He pulled it from his pocket, along with his leaver's certificate, folded into a crumpled square. "Here."

Josh took the book voucher and smoothed it flat. He was going to buy a special book with it, to remind him of George. "Thank you," he said.

"It's OK. When shall I come round?"

"Tomorrow?"

"Got to go shopping with my mum first, but after that?"

Josh nodded. "I'll be home all day—" he sighed dramatically "—on my own."

"You could always see if Shaunna wants to play out," George teased.

"She's going on holiday." Josh's cheeks were turning pink again. He could feel them getting hotter and hotter.

"Oh, well. Just you and me then," George said with a smile.

"Yes." Josh smiled back. "Just you and me."

George
(aged 11)

D O YOU KEEP a diary, George?"
George glanced up from the map—they were discussing where to go on their next bike ride—and saw the circles of pink forming on Josh's cheeks. It probably meant Josh hadn't intended to ask the question out loud.

"No," George answered and switched back to talking about their bike ride to save Josh further embarrassment. "We could always go to the canal again."

"OK." Josh bolted from the room.

George listened to the sounds now coming from the kitchen; Josh was collecting the stuff for their packed lunch.

"You want a hand?"

"No, it's OK. You could check our tyres."

George got up and went outside to do as suggested. Their bikes were standing against the side of the house, one behind the other. Josh's bike was spotlessly clean, and the green paintwork sparkled in the morning sun. George's bike was...well, definitely not sparkling. For a start, it was caked in mud from their ride through the woods two days ago, but even if it had been clean, it would still have been a rusted heap.

It hadn't rusted overnight. He knew that. But like a lot of things recently, he hadn't noticed it before. Like how often Josh blushed, and the way it made his eyes turn the colour of the gemstone in Mam's engagement ring. She didn't wear the ring anymore—*don't want nothing of his, Georgie*—but he could still remember it. Topaz, she'd called it. Blue topaz. He wasn't going to tell Josh that, though. He might think George wanted him to be his boyfriend, when he'd already decided he wasn't going to have one, ever. Or not until he was a teenager, maybe even older than that.

The night before, George had been out on their little balcony, hanging his football socks on the line, when he'd heard shouting from below. Two teenagers, a boy and a girl, were having an argument. They didn't know he was there. He felt guilty about spying on them, and he told himself to look away, to stop listening, but he couldn't help it. The boy kept going after the girl and saying, "I'm sorry," but she turned her back on him. Her face was blotchy from crying, and the boy looked like he wanted to cry too. It was like when Mam kicked Dad out, or Dad walked out, George had never known which it was.

What Josh had said—about it getting easier when you're older—George didn't think it was true. Not for teenagers or grown-ups. Josh was his best friend, and they never argued or had to say sorry or made each other cry. Why couldn't it stay like that forever? *It must be the kissing and other stuff that messes everything up.*

"Are you looking for the pump?"

Josh's question startled George from his thoughts.

"It's there," Josh said, pointing to his bike.

George stared hard at the pump neatly running along the shiny green crossbar. "Would your grandma be OK with me using the hose?"

"Why?"

"To wash my bike."

"Oh. Yes, probably. I'll go and ask her." Josh returned inside but came straight back out again. "You do mean now, don't you?"

George nodded. Josh left a second time.

It wasn't going to make much difference, cleaning the mud off. It would still be old and rusty. George's dad bought his last new bike for him when he was seven. It was a BMX with red tyres, red saddle, red handlebar grips—even the brake cables were red— and a silver body. He'd loved that bike and looked after it. He had his own little oil can for the chain and spray oil for the wheels and spokes.

When they moved to the flat, George had watched the older boys doing tricks on the walls between the buildings and asked his mum if he was allowed to play out with them. She'd said yes and followed him out, to talk to the lads—*look after him, or you'll have me to answer to.* Then she'd stood on the balcony, watching them, and George had felt more like a four-year-old than an eight-year-old. They were big lads, much older than him, or so it seemed at the time. Now he was their age, and they were all fourteen and fifteen. They didn't go out on their bikes anymore— probably too busy kissing girls and having arguments.

"She said yes."

Again, George jumped at Josh's sudden appearance. "Do you have to sneak up on me?"

"I didn't sneak up. You were daydreaming."

George couldn't argue with that. He followed Josh through the gate at the side of the house, across the garden to the outside tap.

"My grandma says we've got to empty the hose afterwards," Josh said.

"How do you empty a hose?"

"Erm…" Josh studied the coiled pipe for a moment and shook his head. "I'll work it out."

"I'm sure you will."

"I will!" Josh protested.

George laughed. "That's what I said, isn't it?"

"Oh. You weren't teasing me?"

George instantly stopped laughing. "No. I'd never tease you about being clever."

Josh blinked rapidly, like he was going to cry.

"Josh?"

"It would be easier if you brought your bike here."

"Are you OK?"

Josh nodded and flashed a smile George's way. "I'll tell you later. Get your bike."

"Why don't you—"

"George."

21

George huffed but did as Josh had told him and brought his bike through to the garden, in time to see Josh disappear through the back door to the house.

"Just getting the brush and shampoo," he called.

Bikes have shampoo? George thought that very unlikely, but a couple of minutes later, Josh returned with a bucket, two scrubbing brushes and, sure enough, a bottle of bike shampoo.

"It's got wax in it," Josh explained, half-filling the bucket with water and then tipping a capful of shampoo into it. "It'll stop it from getting rust…ier." He put the cap back on the bottle and set it down on the ground, going cross-eyed as he struggled to lift the now heavy bucket.

Giggling at Josh's funny facial expressions, George went to his assistance, and they carried the bucket over to the bikes together. Almost as if his bike knew what was in store, a flake of orange-brown paint detached itself from the front wheel fork and wafted to the ground like a dead moth. George sagged. "I'm not sure there's anything left other than rust."

Josh dipped one of the brushes into the bucket and handed it over. "Best not scrub too hard, then."

George took the brush and started at the back of his bike—which was the muddiest end—while Josh started at the front. The shampoo was very frothy, and soon all George could see was brown gloop.

"Use more water," Josh advised, dipping his brush in the bucket again. He'd already cleaned the handlebars *and* the front wheel, and George hadn't even finished the rear mud guard.

Josh was right, though; with more water, the mud easily dissolved, leaving a murky puddle on the flagstones, which Josh rinsed away with the last bit of water in the bucket. He attached one end of the hose to the tap and passed the other end to George.

"Ready?"

George nodded, and Josh turned on the tap. Water spurted from the pipe, hitting the bike with force and spraying muddy suds in their faces.

"Yuck!" Josh took off his glasses and wiped his cheek, leaving a dark smear all the way down to his chin. George tried to keep his eyes on what he was doing, but they kept straying to Josh's dirty face, and every time they did, the hose veered away from his bike.

Josh put his glasses back on and grabbed the hose. "You'd best let me do it, or we'll be drenched."

George refused to let go of the hose, and so they both held it, giggling each time they pulled in opposite directions.

"We'll never get out at this rate," Josh said.

George shrugged. "I don't mind staying in." He turned his head so he could see Josh, once again drawn to the muddy smudge that he desperately wanted to wipe from Josh's cheek.

"You're staring at me."

"You've got mud on your face."

"Where?"

George pointed. "There."

Josh put his fingers into the stream of water and rubbed at his face. "Gone?" George shook his head. Josh rubbed some more. "Now?" George kept on shaking his head. Josh sighed. "You do it."

George wet his fingers and smoothed them over Josh's cheek, taking his time to ensure he removed all of the mud. He knew what a fusspot Josh could be, and if he discovered George had missed any, he'd go mad.

"You've got strong hands."

"They're the same as always."

"I know, but I'd forgotten."

George looked at Josh doubtfully. He never forgot anything. Josh smiled and took hold of George's hand, moving it away from his cheek but not letting go. "I miss holding your hand, George. Sometimes it feels like we aren't best friends anymore."

"But we are."

"Do you promise?"

"I promise."

Josh released him and turned off the tap. "I've been thinking," he said. He disconnected the hose.

George waited with his breath held, unsure if he wanted to know what Josh had been thinking. *What if he wants to be boyfriends instead of best friends? Will we start having arguments? Will we have to…kiss? Ugh.*

"If I take one end of the hose down to the bottom of the garden, and you stay here with the other end and hold it up in the air, the water will drain out due to gravity."

Not kissing. Phew!

"OK," George agreed. Josh took the end of the hose and walked down the garden, the rest of the coiled heap unravelling, with George shouting "Wait!" whenever the hose twisted and kinked, and "OK!" once he'd straightened it out.

He wouldn't have minded Josh being his boyfriend. Not really. He never got bored with him, and he missed them holding hands just as much as Josh did. It was the rest of it—the hugging and kissing—which Josh said was what people did when they were in love with each other. George wasn't in love with Josh, he didn't think, although he wasn't sure what that felt like. It was more… what it would be like to have a brother but without the fighting. Dan had two big brothers, both in high school, and he fought with them all the time. Especially Andy, who was only a year older than them. But even though Dan and Andy got into a lot of fights, they still stuck up for each other. They still loved each other.

Josh was on his way back, winding the hose over his shoulder as he walked. He stopped in front of George. Keeping his eyes on the hose, he said, "I'm a bit jealous of Dan."

"I was…" George trailed off. He'd been about to tell Josh that he'd been thinking about Dan, and he was glad he'd managed to stop himself from saying it. Josh was blushing again and looked very troubled. "Why are you jealous of Dan?"

"It's silly."

"Because of football?" George asked. Josh kept his head down and nodded. "Did you want to play too?" George made the question sound as serious as he could, hoping it would make Josh laugh. It didn't work. "Tell me why."

"You're good at football, and you've got lots of friends—"

"Because I'm good at football," George pointed out.

"What if you make a new friend, and they…become…"

"No." George pulled the hose off Josh's shoulder and put it back on the hook where it belonged. He turned back and took Josh's hand in his. "I will never have another friend like you."

"You can't say that. You don't know who you'll meet in your life. And what if I die?"

"Why would you die?"

"I might."

"You're not going to."

"Everyone dies, George."

"OK. You're not going to for a long time."

Josh scowled sulkily, as he always did when he thought George had outsmarted him. Even though Josh was the cleverest pupil in their school, there were lots of things he didn't understand, like when it was better not to say what he was thinking and how to make new friends. So George sort of got why Josh was worried about football and the other boys George was friends with. The only other child Josh had ever spoken to was Shaunna, and he'd mentioned quite a few times the friendship promise she'd made him on the last day of juniors. It gave George an idea.

Keeping hold of Josh with one hand, he lifted his other hand and extended his pinky finger.

"What are you doing?" Josh asked.

George wiggled his finger. Josh blushed even more and stayed as he was. "Fine," George said. He let go of Josh's other hand so he could link their little fingers together. "Ready?"

Josh's lips twitched. He was trying not to smile.

George took a deep breath.

> *"Best friends, best friends,*
> *Never ever break friends.*
> *If you do, I'll never forget you.*
> *And hope you'll never forget me too."*

"Either," Josh corrected with a grin.

"I know, but then it wouldn't rhyme. Do you feel better now?"

"Yes. Can we go on our bike ride?"

George laughed. "Yeah. Come on."

***

It was quite an overcast day, but dry, so they packed their cagoules, along with their lunch, into Josh's panniers and set off along the canal bank, getting off their bikes whenever they passed other people. George loved days like this when there were lots of people out walking their dogs. They had a little black Scotty dog at home called Nero. Mam had wanted to call him Negro, and she wasn't being racist—it was what was on the inside that mattered, she said—but no way was George shouting that when he wanted the dog to come back, and he had to shout him quite a lot. Nero was only six months old but definitely ready to have his bits and bobs chopped off.

When they first got the dog, George had told Josh what his mum was thinking of naming him, and it was Josh who suggested Nero, as it was the Italian word for black. George put it to his mum—carefully and with a cup of tea at the ready—and she said it actually suited the dog better, seeing as he thought he ruled the world. George wasn't sure what she meant, and he kept forgetting to ask Josh. He was bound to know. *Maybe when we stop for a rest today*, George thought, but it would probably have slipped his mind by then.

George loved all dogs, but if he were to choose one, he'd have gone for a big dog, like a German shepherd or a pointer. There were lots of German shepherds at the rescue where they got Nero, but their flat was too small, Mam said.

They didn't cycle very far today—down to the bridge past the double lock, where they stopped for a while to watch the swans. Last summer, when they first cycled down here, George had noticed the female had a black dot on her beak, so he knew these were the same two swans, and this year they had three babies, although they weren't babies anymore. Soon they'd leave their parents and go off in search of their mates, which was exciting, but sad too.

A boat was working its way through the locks, and the swans climbed up onto the bank, a little too close for safety. George and Josh picked up their bikes and set off back the way they had come, stopping at the viaduct even though it wasn't sunny or raining. They clambered up the slope and lay side by side, listening to the clang of the lock gate closing and the boat chugging onwards.

"When I die," Josh began.

George sighed. "You're not going to die."

"Fine." Josh clarified, "When I *eventually* die, I want you to have my diaries."

George didn't answer for a while. It was hard to imagine someone dying. For him, at any rate. Like with his dad leaving, there was always a chance he'd come back, although his dad didn't know where they lived. But he was still out there, somewhere. Josh's parents were never coming back, and George couldn't get his head around how that must feel.

"Are your diaries about your parents?" he asked.

"The first one is. The others are about everything—school, my grandma, you and me…"

"Is that why you asked if I've got a diary? Because you wanted to give me yours?"

"No. I was just trying to find out if keeping a diary was one of my strange things."

"OK."

"Is it?"

"Dunno."

"Oh." Josh rolled onto his side, facing George. Staring at him. "When you *eventually* die…"

"I haven't got anything to give you."

"You already gave me things to remember you by."

George frowned. "Did I?"

"You gave me your book voucher, and I bought us a copy of *Great Expectations*. And you gave me your friendship promise."

"Oh yeah." George smiled at that. A car passed overhead, sending a judder through the concrete slope. George closed his eyes and focused on the feeling of the vibrations, imagining a spaceship slowly descending onto the road above, setting down its landing struts. *Pshhhh.* The door opens, and…

"You can have my bike," he said, glancing Josh's way. "When I *eventually* die."

"You're not going to die," Josh said.

"Are you saying you don't want my bike?"

"Well, it's, erm…"

"A rusty heap," George finished.

"Yes. It is. But that's beside the point."

"I was only joking."

"I *do* want your bike."

"You don't have to accept."

"Give me the bike."

"It was a joke."

"Give me the bike, George."

"I'm still alive."

"Put it in your will. 'To Josh Sandison, I leave my rusty push bike.'"

"It'll probably have gone to the rag-and-bone man by then."

"Then I'll sue your estate."

"What's that mean?"

"Your children will have to give me money."

"What if I don't have any children?"

"Doesn't matter. The bike's mine. You just said so."

George scratched his head, bamboozled by the weird turn of their conversation. Although it wasn't really a conversation. It was…

"Are we arguing over a rusty bike?"

"*My* rusty bike. Yes."

George lay back, closed his eyes and smiled. "Good."

George
(aged 12)

GEORGE WAS FURIOUS, with himself as much as with the bike thief. He'd only been in the shop two minutes, tops, but it was time enough for someone to grab his bike and be long gone. He set off for home on foot, scuffing his shoes along the pavement in misery. From now on, he was going to have to walk his paper round, which meant he'd be late for school. Maybe the thieving little git would feel guilty and bring his bike back, though somehow he doubted it.

Who would want his scruffy old bike anyway? The front wheel was buckled, and the brakes only sort of worked. George peered down the alleys and walkways between the houses in case it had already been dumped. His empty paper bag was itching his neck, and he took it off, letting it drag along the pavement. *Shuff, shuff. Shuff, shuff.* Mam was going to go mad. There was no way she'd get him a new bike for his birthday, which was still over a month away, and in any case it was after the Easter holidays. So much for bike rides with Josh.

It was five minutes before school started when George left the house, and it was a half-hour walk, although it was second-year assembly, and Mr. Barton probably wouldn't notice George was missing. If he went straight to first period—he checked his timetable and found out it was history—he might get away with it for today, and in future he could start his paper round half an hour earlier. That way, he'd get to Josh's in time for the walk to school. They didn't cycle to school. They didn't always finish at the same time, and if he was on his own, Josh got the bus home.

High school was all right, really. The lessons were interesting, although some of the teachers were cranks. Some, like George's form tutor—Mr. Barton—were really strict, but funny too. It was mad the way he let them get away with the big stuff, like not having their planners, but put them in detention for having their ties done the wrong way around. George had got lucky, though. Some of the other form tutors just took the register and ignored their form the rest of the time, while others— like Josh's—mollycoddled them. George had Josh's form tutor for science, and she talked down to them, like they were still in infants, whereas Mr. Barton treated them like adults.

George couldn't believe he and Josh had been put in different forms at high school. After being in the same class for most of juniors, he still wasn't used to not seeing each other all day, every day. George thought it was probably a bit easier for him than it was for Josh, with him being so shy and hardly ever talking to anyone. Plus, there were a few people from their primary school in George's form. Dan was, as well as some lads they knew from football matches. At first, it had been weird playing on the same team, but they'd played together for almost two seasons now, and they'd had plenty of time to bond.

Shaunna and Adele were in George's form too. Everyone had been put in a form with at least one of their friends from primary school, except Josh. He said it was because he was clever, and he wasn't showing off. He never showed off about being clever. He wanted to be ordinary. All the pupils in his form were clever, so at least he didn't stand out as 'special' there, but they only had one term of second year left, and still Josh hadn't made any new friends.

With football and extra classes and being in different forms, the only time they got to spend together these days was weekends and holidays. Now the evenings were getting lighter, they might get a bit more time, but it meant George always going to Josh's house because he couldn't take Josh back to the flat. Mam worked, and she got grumpy when she was tired, so George didn't ask—

for that reason, mostly. But also because he didn't want Josh to know where he lived.

Before George's dad left, they'd had a nice house with a garden, and sometimes George would have friends round for tea, but they were only ever interested in meeting his dad, and his dad was never there. If he'd known Josh back then, he was certain Josh wouldn't have cared at all about meeting Jack Morley, but George hadn't mentioned who his dad was, just in case. The boys he played football with sometimes remarked on George's surname being Morley, but only Dan had asked him straight out if he was related to 'the famous footballer', and George had answered honestly. Dan said he wouldn't tell anyone. That was years ago, and it seemed Dan had kept his word.

George didn't like having secrets from Josh. They'd been best friends for a long time—almost five years—and George had told Josh some of his biggest secrets, although not on purpose, because his very biggest secret wasn't a secret at all until Mrs. Kinkade talked to Josh about how society frowned upon boys holding hands. Josh had said it was to do with girls and boys being treated differently, and for a while after, they had stopped.

Sometimes, though, at story time, Josh had been so absorbed he would reach out and grab George's hand, not even knowing he'd done it. It was only when the story ended that he'd realise and turn bright pink. He'd always said sorry, and George had always told him it was OK. But then the other children had started to look at them like they were doing something naughty. Right up until they finished juniors, they'd still held hands when they were alone, like if they were watching a film at Josh's house or if they went to the viaduct for a rest on their bike rides. But otherwise, they'd had to stop doing it in front of everyone else.

In the last Christmas holidays before high school, they were at Josh's house. They'd watched *Bedknobs and Broomsticks* and eaten nearly all of Josh's Christmas chocolate in one go. It was fun, even though they'd both felt really sick and Josh's grandma had kept looking at them sternly because they'd been chattering and giggling too much, but they'd seen the film lots of times. When it had finished, they'd talked about growing up and how, when you're little, you hold hands with your best friend, but even the girls didn't do it anymore.

George had hated that conversation. For the first time, he'd understood something about himself that made him as different from everyone else as Josh was. Worse than that, he was different from Josh. Even though they *were* best friends, that was the only reason Josh had liked holding George's hand, but George had started to feel differently about it. Whenever the other children talked about growing up, the girls were always going to marry boys, and the boys were going to marry girls. George didn't want to marry a girl. He wasn't sure he wanted to marry a boy either, but sometimes he'd wonder what it would be like to kiss someone, and he didn't want to kiss a girl.

The best thing about being friends with Josh was that George had never had to say it out loud. He knew the word for it now. He was gay. It had taken him until he was in high school to properly understand what that meant, but Josh had always known and accepted that George liked boys.

Josh didn't seem to like anyone, not even enough to want to be friends, never mind fancying them. But then, Josh was a year younger than everyone else. Sometimes George's voice went funny, and Josh said it was breaking, which meant he'd reached puberty, and George had noticed his body was changing in some places. He didn't like to ask if the same thing was happening to Josh.

With all his thinking, George had walked fast, and he was only twenty-five minutes late for school. He went straight to class, and no-one noticed a thing, or the teachers didn't. Some of the other pupils eyed him suspiciously all morning. He didn't see Josh until they met up in the canteen at lunchtime. Josh gave George a look to ask him why he hadn't turned up for the walk to school.

"Someone stole my bike," George explained quietly as they queued at the serving counter.

"Oh no! When?"

"This morning from the newsagent's. I went in to give them money off someone on my round, and when I came out, my bike was gone."

"Didn't you lock it?"

"No. The lock got nicked ages ago."

Josh frowned. "They stole the lock but left your bike?"

"The lock slipped off while I was riding home from yours. I went back, but some lads ran off with it."

Josh shook his head. "Anyone would think you lived in the Bronx or something."

"Isn't that in America?"

"Erm, yes. But I mean, oh…you know what I mean."

"And now we can't go cycling at Easter."

"True. But we can go for walks."

George shrugged. He was happy to do whatever Josh wanted to, but he was fed up about his bike, and he was dreading going home. *I might not tell her. She probably won't even notice.*

They sat together to eat lunch at the empty end of a table full of fifth years.

"I talked to someone in my class today," Josh said.

"Did you?"

"Yes. A girl called Ellie. She's nice."

"Ellie who?"

"Davenport. Do you know her?"

George thought for a moment. "No, but I think her little brother plays football."

"What's his name? I'll ask her."

"Ben. He's two years below us—at Parkside."

"That's where Ellie went. She wants to be a doctor."

"Oh, right." George tried to think of something else to say, but he felt weird. He was pleased Josh had talked to someone at last, or he thought he was pleased.

Josh was keeping his head down, picking at his lunch. He always chose the same thing: a ham sandwich and a packet of ready-salted crisps. He'd peel the sandwich apart and carefully spread crisps over the ham. Then he'd put the bread back on top and squash the whole thing flat with his hand.

"That's good," George managed eventually.

Josh gave him a quick smile and continued eating. His glasses had slipped down his nose, and they were obviously annoying him, but he had grease and crumbs on his hands. He scowled and flicked his head back. His glasses stayed where they were. George reached across the table and pushed them back in place, hooking Josh's hair out from behind them. His finger brushed across Josh's forehead.

"Thanks," Josh muttered.

George pulled his hand away and put it in his lap. His hand was shaking.

"George!" Dan called. He stopped next to their table and grinned. "Footy?"

"Um, not today. I feel sick."

Dan gave him a firm nod. "Tomorrow then?"

George nodded back and watched Dan collect the other lads on his way to the door. Josh watched too. The lights picked out the soft pale fuzz on Josh's face, the straight slope of his nose, the flutter of blonde lashes behind his glasses, and as he swallowed the food in his mouth, his lips parted. He spun back to face George, and George quickly looked away.

"Do you?" Josh asked.

"What?"

"Feel sick."

"Oh. Sort of." George glanced up briefly. Josh raised his eyebrows. "I'm worried about telling my mum, and…" He didn't finish, but what he wanted to say was *I'd rather sit with you than play football.*

"It's not your fault your bike got stolen," Josh reasoned.

"It is, though."

Josh didn't argue, much to George's relief. It was too hard to explain because it wasn't just telling his mum and getting in trouble that was bothering him. What if Josh found someone else to go on bike rides with? Ellie might become his best friend now. George didn't like how that made him feel. He wanted to think about something else.

"Have we got maths this afternoon?" he asked.

"Last lesson. Do you have a match after school?"

"No."

"Good. So, last lesson together and then walk home?"

George smiled. "Yeah." That made him feel much better.

***

For the rest of the week, George missed football practice, instead waiting for Josh on the days he had extra lessons so they could walk home together. After that, he played out with the other lads around his way and only went in at teatime and took his plate to his room. He felt guilty lying to his mum that he had lots of homework, although for the first time ever it meant he got all of it done. It was even worse when she said she was proud of how hard he was working, and he decided he wasn't going to tell her about his bike.

Then, on Saturday morning, after his paper round, George got back to the newsagent's at the same time as his mum arrived to buy cigarettes. At first, she didn't seem to have noticed, but as they walked back to the flat, she said, "Have you broke it?"

"What, Mam?"

"Your bike. Is it broken? Or did it get robbed?"

"Someone took it from outside the shop. I'm sorry."

She took a long, thoughtful draw on her cigarette. "Have a word with Jono, downstairs."

"Jono? Why?"

"He does up old bikes. See how much he wants for one. Eh, you never know, the thief might've tried to flog him yours."

"I've only got my paper-round wages, Mam. I've got a bit saved up, but not enough for a bike."

They arrived home, and his mum patted him on the arm. "Don't worry, lad," she said.

***

The first day of the Easter holidays, George lay in bed, listening to his mum in the kitchen. She was making a cup of tea and talking to the dog. George felt like his life was over. He'd arrived late at school twice, and he'd done something really stupid. He didn't even think until after he'd said it, but when he'd told Mr. Barton he was late because he had to finish his paper round, Mr. Barton told the headmaster, and the headmaster reported George's boss for employing under-thirteens. It didn't matter that George turned thirteen in three weeks' time. The newsagent wasn't going to give him his job back.

So now he had no money and no bike, and he was supposed to be at Josh's house in half an hour. The thought of spending the day together gave him butterflies, but it didn't make him feel any less gloomy. He got out of bed, put on his dressing gown, shuffled to the bathroom and locked himself inside.

"Off to the shops, love," his mum called.

"OK," George replied. He heard the front door close. If she was going shopping this early, it meant there was no bread for toast, and he was starving. He had a few pennies left in his money box. He could get a bar of chocolate on the way to Josh's. It would be better than nothing. His belly rumbled at the thought, and he quickly finished in the bathroom, put on his clothes and left.

George sped up as he passed by the newsagent's. He was probably barred anyway. It didn't matter. There was a sweet shop on the road next to Josh's. They went there all the time, and George always tried to contribute, but Josh paid for most of their sweets. It used to make George feel guilty, until Josh explained that his mum and dad had left him a lot of money and he liked spending it on George. Today, even though he was hungry,

George wanted to buy their sweets. He bought a packet of Love Hearts and was shoving them in his pocket on his way out of the shop, not looking where he was going, when he bumped right into Josh.

"Oh!" Josh said. "Hello! I've come to get our sweets."

George pulled the Love Hearts out of his pocket and held them up. "Me too."

"Great minds…" Josh smiled. "I'll get something else."

George waited while Josh went and picked out a selection of penny sweets and lollipops. He paid for them and returned to George.

"Come on. I've got a surprise for you."

George followed Josh out of the shop and back towards his house. "What kind of surprise?"

"Wait and see." Josh gave him another smile.

"Is it a big surprise or a little one?"

"Not telling you."

"Josh…"

"Shush. You'll see soon enough."

They arrived at the house, and Josh went in first.

"Close your eyes."

"But I—"

"George!"

He huffed and closed his eyes. Josh took his hand and tugged to pull him along the hallway.

"OK. Open them."

George stumbled forward and kept his eyes shut. He didn't want to open them while Josh was still holding his hand.

"George?"

"Mm?"

Josh squeezed his hand and released him. "Open your eyes."

George opened one eye, then the other, and blinked. "What…" He shook his head. "No. You can't—"

"Too late. Also…" Josh grabbed George's hand again and pulled him closer to the new bike leaning against the wall.

"I bought this padlock and chain. It's heavy duty, so there's no way someone could cut through it, and you have to keep the key in the padlock when it's unlocked. The chain will fit around both of our bikes."

"It's too much."

"It isn't. And anyway, I want us to go on bike rides, so it's for both of us, really." Josh gave George a hopeful look.

George sighed. He wasn't going to win, but he didn't like that Josh had spent so much money on him. What did he have to offer in return? A packet of Love Hearts. "I'll get another paper round and pay you back," he said.

"It's a birthday present," Josh argued.

"It's not even a special birthday!"

"Thirteen *is* special."

"It's still too much."

"So…it can be your birthday present for your next few birthdays. How about that?"

George still didn't like it, but maybe that was a bit fairer. "OK. Only if you promise not to buy me anything until…I turn twenty-one."

"Fine."

"I didn't buy you anything."

"You don't need to. Just say thank you so we can go for a ride."

Josh's grandma came into the hall and looked from Josh, to George, to the bike, and back at George. She shrugged.

"Thank you," George said.

***

With their sweets stowed in Josh's panniers, along with a bottle of orange squash, they set off on their bikes. George had to stop a couple of times to adjust the saddle and handlebars. The bike was metallic blue, shiny chrome finish on the brakes and gear lever, with white racer handlebars and fourteen gears. It was an expensive model, he could tell, and bigger than the one that was stolen—big enough to see him through school.

He'd definitely make sure it was always locked up. The lads around his way would snap it up if he left it for even a second. He still couldn't believe Josh had done this, and he had no idea how he was ever going to repay him.

They didn't go too far, just out to the paddocks, where they stopped and chained their bikes together, attaching them to the paddock fence. They stroked the horses and played the Love Hearts game. It consisted of making one of three choices for what they wanted the other person to do with the phrase printed on the next sweet they pulled from the packet: say it—make up a sentence that included the phrase; do it—enact the phrase; or horse it—forfeit the sweet and give it to a horse or pony of their choosing.

George always ended up forfeiting more sweets than Josh, and today it was worse than ever, because the messages seemed to have far greater meaning—*like me, all mine, too much*—the horses got them all.

Josh's last turn, he read the words on his sweet and closed his fingers around it. "Will we always be best friends, George? Even if you get a boyfriend?"

"Of course we will," George promised. "Why? What does the sweet say?"

"Oh, it's rubbish," Josh said. He held out his palm and George read the words: *good pals.*

"Yeah. That is a bit rubbish," he agreed lightly, hoping Josh couldn't sense his disappointment that it didn't say *true love* or *I'm yours.*

It started to rain, so they left the horses and returned to Josh's house, where they spent the rest of the day—and most of those that followed—playing *Dragon Quest* and *Mario* and watching TV. They did get out on their bikes a few times, but mostly the Easter holidays were wet and windy.

At home, George chained his new bike to the pipe in the hall, and it was a week before his mum noticed it.

"Did you rob it?" she asked.

"No!" George answered, horrified. He'd never stolen anything in his life.

"From Jono?" Before he could tell her otherwise, she went on, "Fell off a lorry, by the looks of it. Still, nice bike. Look after this one, eh?" And she never said another word about it.

***

It was the bank holiday weekend in May before the weather was nice enough for them to go on a proper bike ride. Josh made them a packed lunch, and George—who had another paper round, which paid better than his old one—bought the sweets.

"No Love Hearts?" Josh asked, loading their stash into the panniers.

"Sold out," George said. It was true, and he was kind of glad about that. He was starting to have feelings that he wasn't sure he could share with Josh.

They cycled four miles along the canal bank, and it was a lovely ride: lots of boats, people walking their dogs, and they saw the pair of swans, this year with five cygnets. At the next lock, George and Josh stopped for lunch and lay on the grass bank, enjoying the sunshine. It was bright but not too hot, although Josh's uncovered face had turned very pink, and his hair was becoming blonder, as it did every summer.

George's hair was also blonde, lighter than Josh's in winter, but it stayed the same colour all year round. It was very curly, and when it grew, it grew upwards and outwards instead of downwards, so he got it crew cut every few weeks. He liked Josh's hair, especially when it flopped in his face and he tried to blow it out of the way. It never worked, and if his hands were full, George would push Josh's fringe back for him. It was silky smooth and smelled of coconut shampoo.

"What's wrong?" Josh asked, and George realised he'd been staring.

"Just thinking about your hair."

"Is it going lighter?"

"Yeah. Your face is getting a bit burnt. You want to go back?"

Josh nodded, and they set off once more, back along the canal bank to the viaduct. They stopped, chained their bikes together and collected their sweets and drinks before they clambered up the concrete slope. They often had a rest under this viaduct. Not that he'd told Josh, but George liked to think it was *their* secret place that no-one else ever came to. It wasn't special, just a road over the canal. But it got them out of the sun, and it was a good place to rest up before they rode the last mile home.

For a few minutes, they lay on their backs, catching their breath and cooling down. Josh reached into the bag of sweets and pulled out two lollipops. He held one out to George. Sitting up straighter, George took the lollipop, and Josh settled back with his hands behind his head and his knees up, using the traction of his shoes to stop himself from sliding down the slope. He rolled the lollipop around, and the stick slid from one side of his mouth to the other.

George was transfixed. The stick switched sides again. A car rumbled overhead. The sugar left a glossy coating on Josh's lips, and George wondered what they would taste like, how it would feel to press his lips to Josh's and…kiss him. George's heart was hammering at the thought. He wanted to kiss Josh, more than anything else. He wanted to taste the lollipop on his lips, lick the stickiness away. He wanted it so much he couldn't stop watching the stick bobbing. He could reach over and snatch that stick, pluck the sweet from Josh's mouth, and kiss him.

Josh looked at him in puzzlement. Had he said something?

"Huh?" George asked. His cheeks were burning. The moment had passed, and for now the desperate urge to kiss Josh was lost.

***

George replayed that moment all the way home and for days, weeks, months afterwards. He couldn't seem to get the thought out of his head. He had wanted to kiss Josh. He still wanted to kiss him. Did Josh know? Could he tell what George was thinking?

In maths, George got told off for not paying attention, not just once, but every lesson because he wasn't listening or doing his work. He was lost in a daydream where they were back under the viaduct and he'd been bold enough to act on his feelings, and Josh had been shocked at first, but then he'd kissed him back. They were boyfriends—

"We're dropping you to set two for maths, George," their teacher said. "You're not keeping up with the work."

George wanted to die from shame.

"Don't worry," Josh assured him. "I'll help you—if you want me to, that is?"

"Why wouldn't I want you to?"

"Because…you've been acting strangely. Is there someone in our class that you fancy?"

Yes, you, George wanted to say.

"It's OK if there is," Josh said. "We'll still be best friends."

Josh
(aged 13)

A T THE SOUND of the doorbell, Josh quickly closed his diary, locked it back in the vanity case, and went downstairs. He was expecting George, so he was surprised when he opened the door and found it wasn't George at all.

"Hey, Ellie," he greeted. They'd swapped addresses when they first became friends, but he hadn't invited her to come round. The only friend he'd ever let into his house was George. There again, George was the only friend he'd had until last year. Well, other than Shaunna, but they didn't do much more than say 'hi' to each other if they passed in the school corridor.

"Hi, Josh. Jess and I wondered if you wanted to come into town."

"Jess?" Josh glanced past Ellie. Sure enough, Jess from their form was standing at the gate. She waved at Josh. He waved back. "I'm waiting for George, actually."

"He can come, too," Ellie suggested. "We're only going for a look around the shops and milkshakes."

"Erm…OK. I mean, I'll have to ask him if he wants to. When he gets here."

Ellie turned and beckoned to Jess. She'd assumed he was inviting them to wait inside. He didn't have a problem with that. Or he shouldn't have had a problem with it, but…

"Here comes George, now," Josh said, fighting to contain a sigh of relief. George came up the path and stopped next to Ellie and Jess. He smiled politely at both girls and then frowned at Josh.

"George, this is Ellie, who you know, and this is Jess."

"Hi," George said twice. Again he frowned at Josh.

"Ellie and Jess invited us to go into town with them."

"Just to hang around, or…?"

"Window shopping mostly," Jess said. "I need to buy holiday clothes."

"And milkshakes," Ellie added.

George fished in his pocket and withdrew a few coins. On sight, Josh counted how much was there; barely enough for a milkshake.

"Are we walking?" he asked.

"Can do," Ellie answered. Jess nodded in agreement.

George put his money back in his pocket and shook his head. "Why don't you go, Josh? I need to see…someone anyway."

Josh didn't want to go without George. They always spent their Saturday afternoons together. It was one of the only times they had now, and it was going to get worse once the summer break was over. They started their O' Level exam classes in September, and he and George had chosen different subjects.

"Oh, I know what I needed to show you." Josh grabbed George by the arm and pulled him into the house. "Won't be a second," he said to Ellie and Jess, shutting the door on them.

"Joshua, what are you doing?"

"Have you really got to go?"

"I don't have enough money for milkshakes and shopping."

"I'll buy the milkshakes."

"You can't keep doing that."

"Please?"

George scratched his head. He looked worried.

"I'll tell them we can't go," Josh suggested, reaching for the door latch.

"No. Don't do that. They're your friends."

"So? They turned up out of the blue. They can't expect me to drop everything, just like that." Josh opened the door and smiled at Ellie. "Thanks for the invitation, but we're not coming. George and I have other things we prefer to do on a Saturday."

Ellie looked at Jess, and they both burst out laughing.

"What's funny?" Josh asked.

"I told you," Ellie said to Jess.

"Yeah." She grinned at Josh.

"What did she tell you?" he demanded.

"That you're very abrupt."

"Am I?" Behind him, Josh could see George nodding his head and turned to face him. "Am I?"

"Yep. Kind of rude too."

"I am not. I'm...I...I know my own mind, that's all." Josh folded his arms, which made the other three laugh even harder. Josh glared at George.

"Sorry," he spluttered.

"I can't believe you're laughing at me, George. I thought you were my best friend."

"I am!"

"Oh!" Jess said. The laughter stopped. "We thought you were..." She wagged her finger between Josh and George. "You know?"

"No?" Josh said, watching George to see if he knew what Jess was talking about. George was blushing vivid crimson. Josh shrugged in query.

"They thought we were together."

"Together? Like...oh!" Josh nearly choked on his breath and started coughing. "No...we're...just...friends."

"OK." Jess smiled. "We don't care, by the way."

"So, you coming into town, or not?" Ellie asked.

"Yes," George answered for both of them. "Go and get your jacket, Joshua."

Josh did as he was told and had a glass of water while he was at it. When he returned to the front door, George was explaining how they'd first become friends, and he continued telling the story as they walked into town.

It was interesting hearing it from George's perspective. It wasn't that different from how Josh remembered it. In infant school, he'd been moved up a year, because he was 'gifted', and he was too shy to make friends, so he sat on his own in class, and hardly anyone ever spoke to him. Then his dad died, and all of Josh's lunchtimes were spent inside, either sitting with teachers, who gave him extra work to push him, or talking about his mum and dad with Mr. O'Malley.

The day George started their school, all of that changed. Mrs. Kinkade asked George where he'd like to sit, and he'd chosen to sit at Josh's desk. Josh had never asked him why, but he imagined it was due to it being the only one with free chairs. Whatever his reason, George made a lot of effort to talk to Josh, and Josh found he could talk to George more easily than other children. They became friends, then best friends.

The way George told it, Josh was the only boy in the class who made him feel welcome. He'd 'let' him share his desk, shown him how to do the work and helped him find his way around the school. He made Josh sound like a saintly child, and, he supposed, he was always well behaved. He loved school and learning new things, but he also loved having a new friend who wasn't quite so saintly. In fact, George would have been the naughtiest boy in their school if Dan hadn't beaten him to that honour. It was only ever mischief, and he didn't get into fights or anything like that, but other than riding their bikes and eating too many sweets, Josh didn't think he and George had very much else in common.

When they reached the town centre, they went into the department store, and Ellie and Jess wandered around the cosmetics counters.

"Do you want to look at anything?" Josh asked. George shrugged. "CDs?"

"If you like."

Josh led the way to the CDs. He didn't listen to much music, but it was something to do while they waited for the girls. He flipped through the stacks, starting at 'A' and working his way down. George was watching over his shoulder; Josh knew because he could feel George's warm breath on his ear and cheek. He shivered. "Do you think they were guessing?" he asked.

"Who guessing about what?"

"Ellie and Jess, about you and me."

"I dunno. Maybe it's because we're always together at school," George speculated.

"Except we're not anymore," Josh pointed out.

"We walk to school together and spend lunchtimes together."

"I suppose." Josh frowned. "I hope it doesn't stop you getting a…" He didn't want to say it out loud in case anyone heard him. George hadn't told anyone he was gay, and it was not Josh's business to share it.

"I don't think it will," George said. "But if Ellie and Jess bring it up again, I'm going to tell them."

Josh glanced sideways and saw George's pensive expression. "You don't have to."

"I know, but I trust your judgement. If they're worthy to be your friends…"

"As if I know anything about making friends."

"Yeah, you know that thing I said about you being rude?"

"When am I rude?"

"What you just said is like saying we're only friends because I hassled you into it."

"That's not what I meant at all. Although if you hadn't worked so hard to be my friend, then it would have been my loss."

"I didn't work that hard, although…" George stopped talking and picked up a CD.

"What were you going to say?"

"It's silly."

"Tell me anyway."

"I was thinking that maybe the girls could see it, like, I dunno. Because we're at that age where we could mate."

"Mate?" Josh could feel himself turning red. Talking about sex made him uncomfortable.

"Not mate," George backtracked. "Feel attracted to other people."

"I knew what you meant. Sort of."

"All I'm saying is that it makes sense for girls to be able to tell if a boy isn't interested in them."

"But how would they know?"

"No idea. It could be a chemical thing."

"I see. So, are you asking me if I'm gay?"

George swapped the CD for another and held it up in front of his face—his very red face.

"If that's what you're asking, George, then I don't know."

George put the CD down and smiled. "Sorry."

"It's OK. Shall we go and see if they're ready yet?"

George nodded, and they went to the front of the shop to wait at the doors, as they'd arranged beforehand. Josh stood on tiptoes and peered between the counters. He couldn't see the girls anywhere.

"When did you know?" he asked, glancing at George to check he'd understood the question, although it took him a long time to reply.

"When you told me what Mrs. Kinkade said."

"So you've known since you were nine."

"Yeah."

Josh sighed.

"Everyone's different, Josh."

"I can see it in other people, like you and Jess. She's got a boyfriend, and he meets her from class. I can tell, looking at them together. I bet they're doing 'it'."

George's eyebrows rose, and his blush, which had subsided, returned. "How?"

"I don't know. And Ellie...she says she doesn't want a boyfriend, but I can tell she fancies one of the boys in our form. She's shy too—not as bad as me, I don't think."

"So you'd be able to tell if I fancied someone?" George asked. Josh could see George didn't like that idea one bit.

"I doubt it. I know you too well. But I might be able to tell if someone fancies you."

George grinned. "That might come in handy."

"Oh? Do you like someone?"

George's grin stayed in place, but it didn't look real.

"Forget I asked," Josh said and returned to searching the aisles for Ellie and Jess, spotting them soon after. They were on their way back.

"What do you think of this?" Jess asked, wafting her wrist under Josh's nose. He sniffed and pulled away.

"It doesn't suit you."

"This one?" She wafted the other wrist. He wrinkled his nose, and she made a sad face. "I thought that one suited me."

"It does—if you're trying to ward off evil spirits."

Jess shoved him away, and he laughed.

"You shouldn't joke about stuff like that, you know," Ellie said as she stepped into the revolving doors. Jess gave Josh a weary look and stepped into the segment behind Ellie, George the one after that.

"What's wrong with the way we came in?" Josh muttered, watching the doors continue to spin. As the next segment came around, he quickly stepped in, but the doors were slowing down, and he slowed with them. He looked to George in panic.

Push, George mouthed, using his hands to mime. Josh did so and emerged several seconds later, a little disorientated.

"I don't like those doors," he said, stumbling dizzily after his friends.

"Do you like anything?" Jess asked dryly.

"Erm...I like George. Especially his eyes. Have you noticed how green they are?"

George blushed again—he was like a red Belisha beacon today—and shoved his hands in his pockets.

"Where are we going?" Josh asked.

"The café over there," Ellie said, pointing across the street.

Josh squinted over the top of his glasses to see. He and George didn't go out to cafés or the cinema or anything that cost money. Even though Josh could afford it, he'd never wanted to do it enough to have the fight with George, who was too proud to accept handouts, even from his best friend—too proud for Josh to confess to him that he knew the truth about where George lived, and who his dad was. Maybe one day, George would want to talk about it. For now, Josh would keep George's secrets safely locked away with his own.

In the little café, they ordered four chocolate milkshakes and were told to find a table. Their drinks would be brought over to them. A table became free, and they quickly claimed it.

"Wow, this place is busy." Josh looked around him at all the different people—some their age, most families with young children, plus an older couple. They kept his attention for a while, with their light laughter and fleeting eye contact. "First date," he said.

Ellie frowned and looked where he was looking. She tutted and turned to George. "Does he do this with you?"

"Yep, though we don't often go to places where there are people."

"There are people *everywhere*," Jess pointed out.

"What do I do?" Josh asked.

"Stare," Ellie and George said at the same time.

"I'm not staring, I'm *observing*. I'm going to study psychology at university."

"You need to be more subtle," Jess suggested. "Pretend you're reading a book or something."

Josh smiled sweetly. "Then you won't know when I'm watching you and your *boyfriend*."

"He's not my boyfriend."

"Really?"

"Really." Jess folded her arms defensively. "I do like him, though."

"He likes you too."

"Yeah, right. He's a fifth year."

"Everyone likes you, Jess."

"No they don't."

"Yes, they do. Because you've got erm…" Josh nodded at Jess's breasts. "Those."

"That's not liking me, is it?"

"They're part of you."

"It's all boys see. Not my brain."

"You could always buy a big hat."

"What good would that do?"

"Well, you wear low-cut tops, so you're actually drawing attention to…those. If you wore a big hat—"

"What do you think, George?" Jess interrupted.

"About the big hat?"

Jess rolled her eyes. "Did you notice my boobs?"

"Do I have to answer that?"

"You don't, but I'd be interested to know, with you being a boy."

"I'm a boy," Josh protested.

"Yeah, no offence, but you don't count."

"Why not?"

"Because."

Josh opened his mouth and closed it again. Apart from that one day last year, when he and Ellie had gone to Jess's to work on a school project, he only knew Jess from form time. But, he supposed, he'd started it by mentioning her breasts. Or not mentioning them. He couldn't quite bring himself to say the word.

"I noticed them," George admitted.

"But you're not staring at them," Jess said.

"Nope."

"So, does that mean once you get to know me, they don't stand out as much?"

"Possibly?"

"Do you think I'm pretty?"

"You're vain," Josh said.

"My looks are important. I'm going to be a lawyer, and it's a male-dominated career."

"How does being pretty help?"

"I'll be able to fool them into thinking I'm a dumb blonde and then wipe the floor with them." Jess gave Josh a smug grin. He nodded.

"I like your thinking."

"You do?"

"Yes. What you're trying to establish is how long the window of opportunity stays open."

"Exactly."

"You need to test it on a few more boys."

Jess licked her lips in what Josh assumed was a sultry way. "I plan to," she said, "but I thought I'd see what you two thought first."

"There's no point asking me. I'm a late developer."

"OK." Jess turned her attention to George again.

"I'm...not into boobs," he said cagily.

Jess winked. "Maybe in future we can compare notes."

Their milkshakes arrived, saving George from further interrogation, but it seemed he'd done what he'd said he would and told Jess in a roundabout way. Neither of the girls seemed to care much, both now focused on drinking their milkshakes, which were delicious. They were made with ice cream and went down far too quickly.

Afterwards, the four of them engaged in more window shopping, which consisted of Jess and George enthusing over holiday clothes for Jess, while Ellie and Josh followed them around. Josh was a little forlorn, and he thought Ellie was probably feeling the same way.

"You and Jess were friends at primary school, weren't you?" he asked when once again they found themselves abandoned to the pursuit of the perfect bikini.

"Yeah, but we didn't see each other much out of school. I don't know how we ended up doing this today, to be honest. She usually goes shopping with her mum. She's spoilt rotten."

"I got that impression. Is she an only child?"

"She is, but I don't think that's why her parents spoil her. Her baby sister died."

"So Jess is getting the love for both of them," Josh thought aloud. "That must be quite stifling."

"Probably. Has George got any brothers and sisters?"

"No. It's just him and his mum. His dad walked out on them. That's when he transferred to my primary school."

"Did you know he was gay?"

"Yes. I've always known."

"And you don't care?"

"Why should I? It doesn't make him any better or worse a friend."

"Doesn't it complicate things? Say if he liked you?"

"He doesn't. Not like that."

Ellie's eyebrows flicked upwards for the briefest moment. Whether she'd intentionally blocked her thoughts on the matter, Josh wasn't sure, but she didn't say anything else about George. She didn't need to. She'd planted the seed in Josh's mind.

George
(aged 14)

I<small>T'S NOT VERY</small> exciting, is it?"

"Hm?" George was so engrossed in the oil-painted landscape, he couldn't even tear his gaze from it to see who had asked the question, although he recognised the voice. Well spoken, with a hint of a non-English accent, it belonged to Kris Johansson: one of the three other boys in his Art O' Level class.

"Or, should I say—" Kris drew up alongside George and squinted at the painting "—*I* don't think it's very exciting. It's obviously a matter of taste. Can you see something I can't?"

"What d'you mean?"

"You've been staring at this same picture of a field for the past fifteen minutes."

"Have I?" George knew he'd been studying the painting for a while. The subject matter wasn't that interesting—a bridge over a spring in the foreground, with fields and trees extending to the horizon. But the way the artist had used colour and texture to add depth to the scene was what fascinated George—the darker colours, or not darker, less vibrant, with less detail—and he was trying to memorise the different techniques so he could practise them later.

"OK. Maybe not fifteen minutes," Kris conceded. "But a long time. What do you think of those portraits?" He thumbed over his shoulder to the far end of the gallery.

With much effort, George dragged himself away from the landscape and turned to look where Kris had indicated. Their art class had come to the gallery on a school trip. Most of the pupils had become bored long ago and were huddled on the bench seat running through the centre of the sculpture room.

"I adore the one at the end," Kris said, already moving in that direction but slowly, to give George a chance to join him, which he did, and the two of them strolled over to the portrait. It was of a young man's head and shoulders. He was slim with long, brown hair, long nose and long chin—everything about him was stretched, almost out of proportion. The painting was Elizabethan, yet the man didn't have a beard, just the lightest shadow of new facial hair on his top lip. He must have been around their age.

"He's beautiful, don't you think?" Kris asked.

George nodded in agreement, although he thought 'handsome' was a more accurate way to describe the man's elongated, angular features.

"And the drape of the fabric around his neck…" Kris made a sweeping motion with his hand, following the contours of the chocolate-brown silk scarf. "Doesn't it make you want to unwind it and brush your fingers…"

Kris stopped talking, and George heard him swallow heavily. He'd had a feeling something like this was going to happen. Until a month ago, when they'd started art lessons together, George and Kris had never spoken. They were in different forms and different classes for every other subject. Prior to that, George had only known Kris existed for two reasons, the first being that he was friends with Dan, which meant he sometimes hung around for after-school football matches.

Kris and Dan's friendship was a bit odd—not that George was criticising or suggesting they couldn't be friends. He was sure people thought the same about him and Josh being friends. Other than enjoying bike rides, they had little in common, and yet being friends was easy. They trusted each other, and there was never any pressure nor reason to pretend to be something they were not.

He guessed Kris and Dan must have had the same kind of friendship, as they seemed to have even less in common again. Dan was sporty, masculine—he already shaved every day—and always had a girlfriend, usually Adele, but they broke up and got back together so often that Josh speculated it was governed by the phases of the moon. It took a while for George to realise he was joking, but whatever. The point was, Dan had girlfriends, whereas—and this was the second reason George knew who he was—Kris was gay.

Back in third year, some of the bitchy girls had started spreading rumours about him because of the way he walked and talked. Kris was tall, slim and good-looking in a very distinct way. He was Swedish, and while he did have a light skin tone and pale-blue eyes, he had brown hair, not blonde, although their art teacher said Kris's profile was 'Nordic'. She'd even made him stand at the front of the classroom and sketched his outline so she could explain what she meant. Kris didn't seem to mind. He'd told George he did some acting out of school, and he was a bit of a show-off, which was probably why, when the girls started their vicious gossiping, he decided the best way to shut them up was to tell them they were right. He was gay, and it was none of their business.

They'd now had twelve art lessons together, and Kris had spoken to George many times, but it had been to ask if he was finished with the paint, if he had a pencil sharpener, or to compliment George's work. Now, with Kris's comment about the boy in the portrait, George realised their previous communications might not have been as innocent as he'd first thought. Maybe he was reading too much into it, but that day he and Josh went for milkshakes with Ellie and Jess kept coming to mind. They'd been able to see it, so why wouldn't Kris see it?

George glanced furtively at him and then to the rest of their class, still congregated on the benches, waiting out the last few minutes of the trip. No-one was paying attention, but George didn't know what to say. Kris's eyes kept shifting from the painting to George, each time studying George's face a little longer, until Kris leaned close and whispered, "He looks a bit like you."

"The minibus is here!" someone from their class called.

"Hallelujah!" someone else said loudly.

Kris made eye contact with George, held it for a few seconds, and then smiled and walked away. George returned to the portrait, but all he saw now was a swirling blur of cream and brown as he tried to make sense of Kris's words and actions. In the distance, he heard their teacher ask, "Is that everyone?" He quickly followed her out to the minibus.

They arrived back at school long after everyone else had left, and George walked home on his own, not that he had any recollection of getting there, and he had to wonder how he'd crossed two main roads without getting run over.

***

The next morning, George arrived at Josh's house for the walk to school.

Josh was already waiting at the gate and studied George intently. "Are you all right?"

George nodded, and they set off, instinctively falling into step, no sound other than their feet hitting the pavement. It was quite a nice morning—or would have been if Josh wasn't still watching him out of the corner of his eye.

"You don't look all right to me," Josh said.

"Kris Johansson."

"Yes?"

"You know you said you'd be able to tell—"

"Yes, he does fancy you."

"How do you know?"

"He's in my English Literature class."

"And?"

"And he's talked to me about you."

"What's he said?"

"Nothing much. He really likes your sketches. I think he was fishing for information. I didn't tell him."

"Thanks."

"George?"

"Hm?" When Josh didn't say anything else, George looked up and saw how serious his expression was.

"I'd never betray your secrets."

"I know. He's worked it out, hasn't he?"

"Yes. Do you like him?"

George thought about it rather than answering the question. He didn't know Kris well enough to say he liked him as a person. Did he fancy him? Yes. Could he imagine kissing him? Far too well.

"You should ask him out," Josh said.

"How are we supposed to go 'out' with each other? You saw what the girls did to him. They forced him to confess."

"It's not a crime, George."

"You know what I mean, and it's not just the girls. If he wasn't best mates with the footy captain, I'm pretty sure the boys would've been giving him a much harder time."

"You could meet up outside of school," Josh reasoned. "Just make sure he understands you don't want people to know about you."

George hated that it had to be so complicated.

"Here's an idea," Josh said. "I'll have lunch with Ellie today. That way, if he's thinking of asking you out—"

"I don't want you to do that."

"You could make it look like you're talking about art. Nobody will know."

"But *we* have lunch together. You and me."

"It won't matter if we miss one day."

George shook his head. He'd got past wanting to kiss Josh a long time ago, but they were still best friends, and if it came to choosing between Josh's friendship and having a boyfriend, then Josh would win, no contest.

They arrived at school and went their separate ways to form time, from there to their first period: geography for George, history for Josh, in the temporary classrooms that stood side by side at one end of the main school building. George kept glancing across from the window of his classroom to Josh's, but Josh was working hard and didn't notice. Next week was half-term break, and they'd already made plans for Halloween. They were a bit old for trick or treat, and Josh's grandma was going away for a couple of days. George had offered to sleep over, but Josh said he'd be all right on his own overnight, so they were going to watch *un*scary videos and buy their own treats instead.

George didn't see Kris the rest of that day, but they had art the following morning—the last day of the half term—and he decided he was going to be brave and 'ask him out' because where George knew for sure that Kris liked boys, Kris was playing a guessing game. On the way to school, George sounded Josh out, and Josh said it was a good idea. Now all George needed was the opportunity to put it into action.

The teacher had asked them to buy sketchbooks, and George had used an entire week's paper-round money to do so. His sketchbook had heavy pages—with a good texture for pencil and charcoal—and lots of them, so hopefully, it would last him for a while.

Their first sketch was a still life of the teacher's pot of pens and pencils, and that was what they worked on for the entire lesson. George loved every second. He was using softer pencils, and the shading on the thick, cream paper was perfection. Before he knew it, the bell sounded for morning break, but he wanted to put the finishing touches to his sketch.

"Can I stay over break, please, Miss?" he asked. The rest of the class had already packed up and were on their way out of the room. He'd been so busy drawing, he'd completely forgotten about talking to Kris.

The teacher glanced down at his drawing. "Excellent work, George."

"Thanks, Miss." George grinned, pleased with it himself.

"Yes, by all means, stay and finish off." She collected her bag and her jacket.

George glanced up to watch her leave, discovering he wasn't on his own. He nodded an acknowledgement at Kris, at the same time feeling the heat rise up his neck, into his face. His heart was racing.

Kris walked back to George's desk and leaned over his shoulder. "Wow, that's really good."

"Thank you. How did yours turn out?"

"Well, I was very happy with it until I saw yours." Kris laughed, and his breath moved George's hair, making him shiver. Kris pulled out the chair next to George's and sat, his knee touching George's outer thigh. There was no mistaking the contact as an accident.

"You know that I'm…" Kris paused, giving George room to respond. He nodded. "Are you?"

"Yeah."

"I like you."

"Same."

Kris released a heavy, shaky sigh. "I've never had a boyfriend before."

"Me neither."

"So…do you, err…want to come to my house one day next week?"

"I was going to ask you the same thing. Well, not exactly the same thing. My mum doesn't like people being at ours."

"I understand," Kris said sympathetically. "My mum and dad are OK about me."

"Oh, no, that's not what I meant. My mum's always known, and she doesn't care as long as I'm happy. It's just…she works long hours." George didn't have anything to add to that statement and wasn't sure where to go next. Had he even accepted Kris's invitation?

"What day?" Kris asked.

"Any except Halloween."

"Monday? I live near St. Mark's school. That's where you went, isn't it?"

"Yeah. How do you know?"

"Dan told me. That's all he said, though. It'll be easier to meet at the school so I can show you how to get to my house."

"OK. Monday at St. Mark's. What time?"

"About eleven? There's only my brother at home during the day."

"Eleven is good for me."

"Great." Kris got up from the chair, pushed it back under the table and then leaned close to George again, this time with his hand resting on George's shoulder. "See you on Monday," he whispered, and left.

**

George arrived at St. Mark's school gate at ten minutes to eleven. After six years of being Josh's best friend, he automatically turned up early to everything, otherwise Josh would fret. They'd had a good talk yesterday. George had been worried about Josh feeling put out, and he told him that. Josh said George was worrying over nothing. Their friendship was as strong as ever. George felt much better for hearing the words, even if they did come with a lecture about making sure he'd brushed his teeth properly and showered and all the other things George always did anyway.

Dead on eleven o'clock, Kris rounded the corner and waved at George, smiling broadly—and a touch nervously—as he crossed the road and stopped in front of him. "Hi. I wasn't sure you'd make it."

"You didn't think I'd turn up?"

"Honestly?" Kris shrugged and shook his head. "Come on. It's this way." They stepped off together. "So you weren't always at the same school as Dan?"

"No. I started in second year of juniors. Were you at Parkside?"

"Unfortunately not. I wanted to go to St. Mark's, but my parents sent me to Harwood Prep."

"The private school?"

"Yeah. It's more like school in Sweden, apparently. And it was OK, other than not being with my friends."

"It's expensive, isn't it?"

"I think so. Lars—my brother—did all of school there. He started university this year. He's home for reading week or something."

George nodded, taking it all in.

"This is where I live." Kris opened one of a pair of wide, wrought iron gates leading up to a big Victorian house. George obediently followed him through and waited for him to shut the gate behind them. "Have you got any brothers and sisters?" Kris asked. He led George up the long driveway, around the side of the house, past a garage and through another gate into the back garden.

"Nope. Just me and my mum," George answered, looking around him in awe. The garden was huge, with rockeries and a pond. There were also lots of trees, two of which were oak trees with thick trunks, their branches full of clusters of acorns, and in the lower branches of one of the oak trees was a small, shed-like structure.

Kris glanced at George and then turned to see what he was looking at. "Ah, the treehouse. It's…very cosy. D'you want to see?"

George nodded dumbly. He'd never been in a treehouse before. He'd never been anywhere like Kris's house before.

"I haven't been in it for a while," Kris explained, climbing the ladder ahead of George. "But Lars was out here with his girlfriend over the summer, so it shouldn't be too damp."

Kris opened the trapdoor in the bottom of the treehouse and clambered through the opening, disappearing from view. Intrigued, George followed.

"This is awesome," he said, genuinely impressed.

"Yeah," Kris agreed wearily, but then it was ordinary to him. "We can stay out here if you like. I'll go and get us some drinks."

"I don't mind."

"We might as well. No-one will disturb us out here, if…" Kris turned red and averted his eyes. "What would you like to drink? A cold drink? I can make coffee or tea?"

"A cold drink is fine. Whatever you're having."

"OK. Won't be long." Kris left.

George used the opportunity to take a good look around. It wasn't a particularly big space—about six feet square, he estimated, based on the size of the mattress taking up most of the floor, with a square cut out of it to accommodate the trapdoor. There were also cushions positioned around the edges of the mattress and plenty of blankets. It was like a miniature log cabin. Branches blocked much of the light coming through the small window, but there was also a strip light halfway up one wall. If they were younger, it would have been a great place to have sleepovers. It could still be, except they probably wouldn't be innocent sleepovers anymore. The thought made George both excited and anxious.

"I've brought us orange juice." Kris's head popped up through the hatch, followed by two glasses and a carton of juice, which George took from him so he could climb with his hands free. "You can sit down," Kris invited. George accepted. Kris poured the juice and handed a glass over, and they drank in awkward silence.

After what seemed an eternity, but was probably no more than two minutes, George said, "How's your sketchbook coming along?"

"Oh…it's…" Kris chewed his lip. "It's shit. I can't draw very well."

"I've not seen your drawings, but your paintings are great."

"Thank you. I'm kind of OK with a paintbrush, but not with a pencil. Do you think Miss would let us sketch in pen?"

"I don't see why not. They're our personal sketchbooks, aren't they? I think she wants us to go with the flow."

"Yes, that's true. How's yours? Full of amazing sketches, I bet."

George thought about the two pictures he'd sketched over the weekend and smiled to himself. They weren't brilliant, and almost nobody else would understand what they meant, but he did, and he was happy with how they'd turned out. He was planning on doing some more work on them later.

"It's going OK," he answered finally.

The silence resumed, and they drank the rest of their juice. George could tell Kris felt as nervous as he did. He was clinging to his empty glass and drumming his fingers against the bottom of it in a steady pattern, like the fast drip-drip-drip of a tap not quite closed off. There was so much tension between them, and it was difficult to know what to do. They should probably talk more, get to know each other first, and *then* think about doing other stuff, but George's gaze kept wandering back to Kris's mouth. Just like under the viaduct with Josh, the urge built, became more intense, took him over…

"Did you want—" Kris's words evaporated as George moved in and kissed him, once, with his lips tightly closed. Kris bounced forward slightly as George moved away, blinking in surprise, his eyes bright, large dark pupils taking over most of the pale blue. He put his glass to one side and climbed onto his knees. George mirrored him, and they kissed again, parting their lips this time.

"Are you sure no-one will come in?" George whispered.

"I can lock the hatch," Kris suggested. George nodded and sat back on his feet while Kris secured the trapdoor. He crawled back to George, and they tumbled sideways onto the mattress.

For a long time, they kissed, explored with their hands, didn't speak. It was fulfilling and frustrating all at once, and it was everything George had imagined it would be. Minus the arguments. Those probably came later.

⁎⁎⁎

"What did you get up to yesterday?" George asked, popping open packets of sweets to fill the large bowl Josh had put on the kitchen table.

"Not much. I went to Ellie's in the afternoon and stayed for dinner."

"Did you have fun?"

"Yes. Sort of. It's a noisy house."

"Why?"

"Well, Ellie's the eldest, then there's Ben—he said hi, by the way—then there's Charlotte, who's nine, Luke, who's seven, Tilly, who's five, and Teddy, the baby."

"Wow. Six of them?"

"Yes. They're Roman Catholics."

"Ah, yeah. I knew that."

"Did you?"

"You told me."

"Did I? I don't remember. It's probably a good idea you don't mention to Ellie you have a boyfriend, though."

George's stomach flipped.

Josh turned slowly and looked him in the eye. "You do have a boyfriend, I take it?"

"Um…" George knew he was blushing and couldn't get his mouth to cooperate, so he answered with a nod.

Josh grinned and picked up the bowl of sweets. "So I shouldn't ask what *you* got up to yesterday, by the looks of it." He walked away, leaving George floundering in the kitchen. He really hoped Josh didn't start asking questions. It meant a lot to have his blessing, but there was no getting past the fact that he was the first boy George had wanted to kiss. George liked Kris, and he definitely wanted to do more of what they'd done yesterday. But he'd also had to do a lot of soul searching, to make sure he wanted to be with Kris for the right reasons and not simply because he couldn't do all the other stuff with Josh.

"Don't forget the lemonade," Josh called. George picked up the bottle and quickly went through to the living room, where Josh had already laid out their sweets and snacks and set up the video. George sat next to him on the sofa and poured the lemonade. "Ready?" Josh asked. George nodded, and Josh pressed play. The title music started, and white writing flashed up on screen.

"We're still OK, aren't we?" George asked.

Josh leaned forward and, without looking, picked two Love Hearts sweets out of the bowl. He gave one to George and kept the other in his hand.

"What's the forfeit?" George asked.

"There isn't one. Say it or do it."

George glanced down at the sweet. "Say it." He grinned and held the sweet up for Josh to read. Josh laughed.

"Yes," he said. "But even if it hadn't told me to 'say yes', the answer would've been yes, we're still OK." Josh flipped over the sweet in his hand. "Do it," he said, holding it up so George could see.

George read it and looked at Josh in confusion. "Really?"

"Yes. If we can't hold hands anymore, we could at least hug sometimes."

"Fair enough." George shuffled along the sofa and put his arms around Josh. "I thought you didn't like being hugged."

"I was wrong."

George
(aged 18)

"Are you up, love?"

George pulled the pillow over his face. No, definitely not, and nowhere near ready to be, either. He tried to pull the covers up, but the dog was on the bottom of the bed. "Geroff, Nero." The dog didn't budge.

"It's gone seven already."

"OK, Mam." He poked one leg out of the side of the bed and groaned.

"*Georgie! Come on!*"

"All right!" George flung the pillow away and sat up. "What on—oh!" Not the dog at all. He grinned. Now he remembered. He got up, stretched, and wandered from the room, still rubbing his eyes as he approached his mum from behind.

"I'll be in with a bucket of water in a minute, lad," she shouted.

"No need," he said right next to her ear. She jumped.

"You beggar." She reached up and pinched his cheek. "Mornin', Georgie. Happy Birthday."

"Thanks, Mam." He wandered away again, to the bathroom and then back to his bedroom for the present and pile of cards. He brought them out to the living room and cleared a space on the couch.

"Here you are, love." His mum put a cup of tea down on the coffee table in front of him. "You'd be best leavin' that lot till you get home from the farm."

"Not working today, Mam. I've got the weekend off."

"Oh, right. You out tonight, then?"

"Going to a friend's. Why?" He knew she wouldn't have planned a surprise party or anything like that. She couldn't afford to, for one thing. For another, his enduring memory of his eighth birthday had been his dad leaving, so it was better they passed by unmarked. But this was his eighteenth birthday, and his friends were having none of that.

"No reason," his mum said, digging in her handbag. She took out her purse and opened it. "Let's have a look."

"Mam…"

"Hush, you." She held out two crinkly ten-pound notes. George sat on his hands. "Take 'em."

"I've got enough already."

"*Take 'em!*"

George scowled but did as he was told. He'd sneak them back into her purse later when she wasn't looking. She could barely afford to live, never mind give him money. If he'd had his way, he'd have been working full time at the farm rather than going to sixth form and only working weekends. It was long days of hard, physical labour for little pay, but he loved it, especially working with the livestock. Whether it was mucking out barns and stables, chasing wayward sheep or shovelling manure, George didn't care. He was physically fit, the work didn't tax his brain, and he'd gladly have spent the rest of his life doing it, but his mum wanted more for him. So he'd got his head down at school and applied for a place at university. All being well, he was off to Aberdeen in September, to do a degree in agricultural studies.

"Are you waitin' for 'em to open themselves?" his mum asked, nodding at the pile of envelopes.

George tutted. "Can I open my present first?"

"It's your birthday. You can do as you like."

He picked up the small, cube-shaped parcel, aware of his mum watching and fidgeting. He ripped the wrapping paper off, revealing a deep-blue hinged box.

"It's not one of them knock-offs what the lads sell," she said.

George had already guessed what was inside and could tell from the quality of the box that it wasn't a fake. He pushed the lid up, and it sprang open with a snap. "Oh, Mam. It's beautiful." He lifted the chunky silver watch free, wound it up and held it close to his ear, using the rapid *tick-tick-tick-tick* as a distraction from his tearful happiness, and the terrible sinking feeling that accompanied it. She'd have bought the watch on lay-away, and it would have cost her a fortune. Now he knew why she'd not been to bingo in weeks.

He got up and hugged her, getting prickled by rollers as he leaned in to plant a sloppy kiss on her cheek. "Thanks, Mam." He fastened the watch around his wrist, twisting it from side to side, admiring it from different angles.

"Cards?" his mum prompted, swiping at her eyes with her sleeve.

George shifted the box and wrapping paper out of the way and set to work on his cards—one from his mum; one from her best friend Pauline; one from his old primary school teacher, Mrs. Kinkade; one from Jono; one from...

"Colorado?" He didn't know anyone in Colorado. He tore open the envelope and pulled the card free. A piece of paper slipped out. It was a short, handwritten letter.

> *George,*
>
> *Sorry for not contacting you sooner. I wanted to get straight before I invited you over to the ranch. I've bought you a little something in preparation – hope it goes some way toward making amends.*
>
> *Happy Birthday.*
>
> *Love,*
> *Dad*

"It's from him, in't it?" his mum asked. George didn't answer. Instead, he shoved the letter back inside the card and gripped the edge of the card between his forefingers and thumbs, all set to rip it to shreds. "Georgie!"

"I don't want his crap, Mam."

"Don't be daft."

"But—"

"But nothin'. Take him for what he's got, love. Eh? What's he sent you?"

George passed over the birthday card, along with the letter and a business card for the livery stables he and Josh had visited countless times since they were little. It was one of their favourite places to go, especially in winter, when it was too cold to cycle along the canal.

"Well, you know what they say, love?" His mum passed the card back to him and winked. "Never look a gift horse in the mouth."

***

"You reckon it's riding lessons, then?" George asked Josh. It was blowing a gale and raining torrentially, so they'd borrowed Josh's grandma's car: a pale-yellow Citroën 2CV, which was ancient and not very speedy, but Josh wasn't a boy racer. He'd only passed his test two months earlier—on his seventeenth birthday—and he was a confident but ultra-careful driver.

"It seems likely, doesn't it? 'A little something in preparation'— unless he's bought you a pony?"

"Hm." From what George could remember of his dad, which wasn't much, that would be typical of him—to think he could undo all the damage with one grand gesture. "I'm not accepting it, whatever it is," he said.

Josh stopped the car outside the stables. "Are you ready?"

"I s'pose." George unclipped his seat belt and left it to slowly retract.

"You can always pretend you didn't get his card," Josh suggested.

"No." George opened the door. "Let's do it."

They walked over to the stable owner's house and knocked, but there was no answer, and after wandering the stables and paddock in the rain for twenty minutes with no signs of human life, they returned to the car.

"Maybe it's a sign," George said, peering at the condensation-misted gloom on the other side of the windscreen. "Shall we just go?"

Josh shrugged and put the key in the ignition, jolting it out again when he jumped in surprise at the sharp rap on the driver's side window. He lowered it.

"All right, lads?" The stable owner smiled at them both and then looked past Josh to George. "Is your surname Morley, by any chance, George?"

He nodded.

"That would explain it. If you come with me, I'll introduce you to her."

"Her?" George and Josh both said at the same time. The stable owner was already halfway to the stables. George and Josh got out of the car again and followed.

She stopped at the end stall and turned back to talk to them. "Now, she was a bit skittish yesterday, but that's just from travelling. She's settled well, though—" she opened the top of the door "—haven't you, Maggy?"

Hook, line, sinker.

That 'little something' was a six-month-old, mixed breed filly with a gorgeous temperament, who shared George and Josh's passion for sweeties—Josh had come armed with 'birthday' Love Hearts. She already responded to the name 'Maggy', and George decided not to change it. He still resented his dad and had no intention of contacting him, never mind visiting him in Colorado, but Maggy instantly won his heart.

George and Josh spent the rest of the day at the stables, grooming Maggy and enjoying each other's company. Through the ups and downs of high school, their friendship had endured, and George knew he could confide in Josh about all the things that were on his mind, stopping him from properly celebrating his eighteenth birthday. Like, for instance, how he still hadn't forgiven Kris for 'betraying' him.

Not that Kris had *actually* betrayed him. They'd gone out with each other for a year, on and off, and they were definitely finished by the time Kris admitted that he wasn't gay, he was bisexual. George hadn't taken it well, and he was being unreasonable.

He knew because Josh had refused to offer an opinion, which meant he didn't agree.

Kris had been open about his sexuality at school, first by coming out as gay, and then having to come out all over again as bisexual. If anyone dared to suggest that he'd only *thought* he was gay, he'd get angry and storm off in tears, and he expected George to support him, to understand, but George didn't understand. What was he? An experiment while Kris figured out who he was? George had never, and nor would he ever, accuse Kris of only *thinking* he was gay. What they'd shared together was real. But he couldn't get his head around bisexuality, and the more Kris tried to explain it, the less sense it made.

George and Kris had argued constantly. They *still* argued constantly, even though they'd not been together for...well, a long time, seeing as Kris had been 'with' Shaunna since Krissi was born, and Krissi was two and a half years old. But George couldn't fault Kris on what he'd done for Shaunna and the baby, especially as Krissi wasn't his. Since Shaunna found out she was pregnant, Kris had supported her in every way he could. And he'd fallen in love with her, which was how he'd concluded he was bisexual.

So Kris was kind of with Shaunna but not, as Shaunna didn't want a relationship. She wanted to prove she was a good mum, which she was, and Kris was doing a pretty decent job of being a good stepdad too.

None of it made George feel any more comfortable about spending his eighteenth birthday at Shaunna's house, but he'd refused to go out, and he definitely didn't want a party. So, he'd been told in no uncertain terms. They were doing pizza and beer or juice, as appropriate, and there would be a cake, and if he didn't like it, tough.

"Are you worried about tonight?" Josh asked.

George laughed. These days it amused rather than surprised him when Josh correctly guessed what was troubling him, and he liked that they knew each other so well. "Yep. I was thinking..." He started clearing away the grooming equipment. "We should celebrate our eighteenth birthdays together next year."

"Yes!" Josh agreed enthusiastically. "We could arrange it for when we come home at Easter."

They finished up in the stable, checked Maggy had plenty of hay and water, and left her with a promise they'd be back tomorrow.

In the car, George put his watch back on.

"That's really stylish," Josh said.

"Yeah. It's from my mum."

"I thought it was."

George ran his finger around the watch face. "I hate him."

"Your dad?"

He nodded. "This watch...my mum...I'm so confused."

"Because you're already attached to Maggy, and you feel guilty for liking your dad's present more."

George sighed. Josh had hit the nail right on the head. "What do I do about it?"

"Whatever feels right."

"I want to keep Maggy."

"Then keep her."

"OK. I will." They fastened their seat belts. "You didn't buy me a present, did you?"

"No. You made me promise not to, remember?"

"I remember." George grinned. "Thank you for the bike. Again."

Josh laughed. "You're welcome. *Again.*" He started the car and slowly moved off.

"And don't think you're going to pay for tonight, either," George added.

"It's already paid for."

"Joshua..."

"Not by me. By everyone."

"But you organised it."

"No. Ellie did."

George had no comeback to that. Back in fifth year, when they'd started to all go out together as a group, he'd noticed Ellie acting strangely. If they went out for a burger or to the cinema or bowling—anywhere there was food—she'd go to the loos as soon as they'd finished eating, and unlike the other girls, she'd make sure she went on her own. George had told Josh, and Josh had borrowed library books about eating disorders. Most of the stuff was about anorexia, which Ellie definitely didn't have, but there was some other stuff about bingeing and purging, which sounded exactly like what she was doing.

The pair of them had spied on her until they'd collected hard evidence—photos taken through her bedroom window, of her bingeing on chocolate—and then they'd confronted her. It was a horrible thing to do, and she hadn't yelled at them, or threatened to call the police. She'd broken down in tears and confessed everything, relieved it was no longer her secret alone. She'd refused to see her doctor but agreed to them helping her, except they had no idea if what they were doing was making her better or worse. The one thing that did seem to help, though, was being in control of what was going on around her, which essentially gave her a free licence to boss them about.

Hence she'd organised tonight.

"So it's all paid for?" George asked.

"Yes."

"Not by you."

"Not by me."

"OK."

They'd arrived back at Josh's house. He stopped the car and pulled on the handbrake. "But I'm paying for our party next year."

"You're not."

"I am."

"Not."

"I bloody well am. *I* can afford to. *You* can't. It's logical, you know it is."

"Fine."

"Fine?"

"Yep." George shrugged. "Fine." He got out of the car and waited for Josh to do the same. "But I'm buying the drinks at the sixth-form ball."

Josh
(aged 17)

SIX A.M. ON a clear day in late June: Josh opened his bedroom curtains and shielded his eyes. The sun was already high above the horizon, casting the rooftops in glorious hues of genuine sunshine yellow. It was magnificent but still a touch too early to be awake on a day that wouldn't end until tomorrow. Josh sat on his bed and breathed deeply, his thoughts soaring up, up, mingling with the wispy cirrus clouds, the only white breaking up the perfect blue sky.

In three months' time, their friendship group would be just as those clouds, stretched, dispersed, by higher education rather than high altitude. Once, they were cumulus, sheep-like, ambling through their primary school days, when learning was fun for everyone. For Josh, that had never changed, though he had witnessed the intellectual struggles of others and tried not to judge them by his own measures.

Shaunna, he did not consider a failure. After all, she had told him on their last day at primary school that reading bored her, and at high school she had gravitated towards the girls to whom she would always be superior—shallow girls concerned only with their looks and in undermining the confidence of others in foolish attempts to better themselves. Josh would never understand why Shaunna had found them appealing, and motherhood, regardless of her tender age, had been her saviour. The friendship vow she had made to him had proved stronger than he'd believed it to be, for seven years on, they were *still* friends. Alas, it counted for nought when it came to persuading Shaunna to leave her almost-three-year-old daughter for just one evening and join them for their sixth-form ball.

Now I have two friends too. How hard it had been to believe back then that he would make more friends, yet tonight, there would be *eight* of them sharing a limousine. Stranger still to think that one of the eight was Dan—the one boy Josh believed was capable of taking George away from him. He wasn't sure he believed that anymore, but the insecurity still reared its head from time to time.

Back in third year of high school, Dan had caught Josh watching the boys take their post-PE-lesson shower, and he'd muttered the word 'queer', but it wasn't like that. Seventeen he might be, but sex was a thing Josh had yet to comprehend. He understood the mechanics—he even understood how sexual attraction worked; he saw it all around him every day. All of his friends, at one time or another, had felt its pull—some less strongly than others—but they *had* still felt it. All except him.

There was only so long he could cling to the 'late developer' theory, and it was making him miserable thinking about it. Better to get moving, properly greet the day.

Down to the kitchen, then, to make coffee and...*not think about cigarettes either.* He'd promised Ellie and George he'd give up, at least until the sixth-form ball, but he was only doing it for George, really. Ellie already had the doctor nag off to a fine art. *One less thing to learn at uni.* George didn't nag. In fact, it was Josh who'd brought it up first.

Do you care that I smoke?

Yes. But it's none of my business.

So the promise was *for* George, rather than *to* George.

Coffee made, drunk. Showered, dressed, out for a walk because that nicotine gremlin was tenacious. Josh turned left and walked, turned right and walked, turned, turned, turned, no route consciously in mind, but his unconscious propelled him to St. Mark's primary school. There, the day was just beginning, a herd of cumuli children trotting after Mrs. Tanner, the immortal lollipop lady, the ferryman's less grim alter ego. The school uniform had changed, Josh noted, and not for the better. Gone were the shirts and ties from his primary school days, in their place pale-blue polo shirts adorned with a modern interpretation of their old school badge.

Progress. Josh supposed there were good reasons that he might even agree with, on a better day, when he hadn't thought himself into a dark hole. He shouldn't be feeling like this. The sixth-form ball was a celebration, the end of an era, the beginning of the rest of their lives, and he was excited about it. But the era that it ended…

Will we always be best friends?

Boyfriends and other friends hadn't come between them, so why should three years at university? He would miss George. Tremendously. He would miss their bike rides, their trips to the sweet shop. They were too old for such things now. Perhaps. Still, they enjoyed nothing more than buying a packet of Love Hearts and visiting Maggy and the other horses.

The school bell called the children inside, and Josh moved on, taking the long way home and dawdling; so many hours to fill with nothing after weeks of cramming for exams. His mind was used to the constant recycling of information, and it refused to return to idling, yet it proved equally resistant to the sustained attention required to read a book, or certainly one of substance. He'd read every romance, thriller and biography in his grandma's collection of novels. Had it been late enough to go to the library, he would have done so. Instead, he turned the corner into his road, faltered a moment, and then quickened his pace. *My sanity is saved.*

"Did you wet the bed, George?"

"I could ask the same of you," George replied, automatically following Josh inside. "I need your help."

"With?"

"Trousers." He brought his hand from behind his back and held up a hanger with his dress trousers clipped to it.

Josh continued through to the kitchen and filled the kettle. "Explain," he said.

"I've grown two inches in the past month."

"No, you haven't."

"My trousers are too short."

"They were too short when you got them."

George started to fidget. He cleared his throat. "Can you, um…sew?"

"You know I can sew. What you mean is, will I sew your trousers."

"Yeah, that's what I mean."

Josh turned to George and looked him up and down. "You have grown a little. Put them on so I can see what I'm dealing with."

George unzipped his jeans and kicked them off, along with his trainers. Josh raised his eyebrows.

"What?"

"My grandma's going to be in for a surprise if she comes in now."

George sped up, tugging his dress trousers free of the hanger and shoving his feet down the narrow legs. He huffed and scowled. "I hate them."

Josh frowned in sympathy. "I know. Do you want to buy a new pair? We could—"

"No." George zipped and fastened his trousers and pointed at the hems. "They can be made longer, can't they?"

Josh crouched down so he could examine the hems. There was an inch, possibly an inch and a half of turn-up he could utilise. "It might be enough," he said. He stood up straight again. "Take them off, and I'll see what I can do."

"Thanks." George sighed in relief.

"If you'd let me pay for—"

"No."

"Fine." Josh left to fetch the sewing box. "Make the coffee."

"Anything you say."

"I'm buying the drinks tonight."

"Apart from that."

Josh smiled. He *would* buy the drinks tonight, for as long as he could get away with it.

"I saw Kris yesterday," George said, handing his trousers to Josh and quickly getting back into his jeans.

"Did you?"

"Yep. Shaunna told him if that limo goes anywhere near her house tonight, she'll never speak to any of us again." George shrugged. "Kris and I will have to pair up."

"Do you want to go with Ellie?" Josh took a small pair of pointed scissors and began snipping away the stitches.

"Best not. I've already upset Kris enough. And as he pointed out last night, no-one's going to think I'm gay by association now, are they?"

Josh kept snipping.

"You believe him."

"I have no opinion." Still snipping.

"After all the grief he gave me about the importance of being open..."

"No opinion whatsoever."

"Oh, come on, Joshua. You *always* have an opinion."

"Not one I'm willing to share with you."

"You think I'm being unreasonable."

"George..."

"How would you feel if your boyfriend demanded you told the school you were gay and then he turned straight?"

"Bisexual."

"Same difference. Now I'm the only *queer*."

"Somehow I doubt that."

George growled with contained rage. That was how it had been for months. He shoved his feet into his trainers.

"Going somewhere?" Josh asked.

"I don't need a lecture."

"Who's lecturing?"

"I know what's coming—'If you're open about it, others will be too. You're not alone, George'—and I'm sick of hearing it."

"I didn't say any of that."

"You *implied* it. Give me my trousers. I'll deal with them myself."

"I said I'd do them."

"Joshua."

"Just go and see Maggy or something."

"If that's what you want."

George stormed out of the house, not quite slamming the door. Even in fury, he was more respectful than that.

***

Six p.m. already: George was cutting it fine. Josh had made the alterations, pressed the new hems and hung George's trousers, ready for his return. He'd expected him to come back an hour or so after his tantrum—*no*, that wasn't the right word. Tantrums were overreactions to trivial matters, and George had every right to be angry, although it was misdirected. Falling for Shaunna wasn't the first time Kris had indicated his attraction to the opposite sex. Josh recalled the argument between George and Kris at the party—the one where Shaunna got pregnant—and it had started with discussing pornography—yet another mystery to Josh. Nonetheless, he could see why to George, Kris's realisation that he was bisexual was a betrayal of sorts, regardless of their relationship being a thing of the past.

By six thirty, Josh was dressed and ready to go. The limousine was picking them up in twenty minutes, and there was still no sign of George. Josh glanced in the mirror hanging in the hallway.

"Damn it." He ran his fingers through his hair and released it. It flopped back over his face.

Upstairs again, Josh tried hairspray first. The humid day had turned his hair flat and lifeless. He lifted a section, sprayed at the roots, and kept hold while he waited for the spray to set. He let go; his hair stuck up on end. He sighed and took off his jacket.

Back to the bathroom, to wash out the failed hairspray; he heard the front door open while he was rinsing off the shampoo.

"You upstairs?" George called.

"Yes. I'll be down shortly. Just washing my hair…" *again.*

"Your trousers are hanging on the coat hooks."

"Got them, thanks."

Josh decided to forego the conditioner and dashed back to his room to dry his hair. It didn't take long to dry, but getting it to do anything more than flop in his face was proving impossible, and time was running out. He turned off the hairdryer and squirted mousse onto the palm of his hand.

"You ready?" George shouted.

"Almost."

"No rush. Adele's having hair trouble too."

"Who says I'm having hair trouble?"

George laughed knowingly and said no more. Josh massaged the mousse into his roots. More drying. Another glance in the mirror—

"Dull as dishwater."

—and back to the bathroom.

"How you doing?" George called.

"Getting there."

"OK. You've got another fifteen minutes. Kris has gone to Shaunna's for one more try."

"Did someone read him his last rites?"

No answer. Josh washed his hair in record time. No messing about this time, just his usual wash, brush, blow dry. If it flopped, it flopped. Nothing he could do was going to stop it. He returned downstairs, where George was leaning against the wall, ankles crossed, hands in pockets, tie unfastened, but his suit now fitted him perfectly. He looked…

"Wow." Josh stopped in his tracks and studied George in wonder. "You're handsome tonight."

"Only tonight?" George teased.

Josh smiled. "Let me guess. You can't tie a bow tie."

"I tried."

Josh made it down the last few steps and across to George. He picked up the two ends of the tie.

"Sorry about this morning," George said.

"It's OK."

"It's not your fault."

"It's fine, really."

"Even so. I shouldn't take it out on you."

"That's what best friends are for. Well, that, and honest opinions on hairstyles."

George shifted his eyes upwards, to Josh's hair. "Looks the same as always."

"I suppose that'll have to do. There. Done." Josh stepped away.

"Thank you. I'm impressed."

"With my bow tie tying?"

"With the lack of flapping at us being late."

"Not much point, is there?"

George nodded and smirked. "I'll have to remember that in future."

Josh stuck out his tongue, which made George laugh. There was a knock at the door.

"That's our ride. You ready?"

"Yes. Oh, one sec." Josh grabbed a pink scarf from the coat hooks and draped it around his neck, over his silver-grey dinner jacket.

"I thought that was your grandma's scarf," George remarked, tongue-in-cheek. Josh opened the front door and shoved George out.

"See you later," he called to his grandma. She didn't respond, which was entirely normal. Theirs was a very quiet house—the antithesis of Ellie's, which was their next port of call.

"Hey, Kris. Love the suit!"

Kris beamed and pushed his rolled-up sleeves a little higher. He looked like a pop star. "Thanks. You two look great."

Josh smiled bashfully and climbed in the back of the limousine. George followed, then Kris.

"No luck with Shaunna?"

"Almost, but no. She's got a dress and everything. It's such a shame."

"We'll have to make sure we enjoy ourselves enough for her too," Josh said, hoping he'd convincingly disguised his sadness. *That's it now. We're friends forever.* Maybe he should have tried to talk Shaunna into coming. Or maybe respecting her decision *was* being a good friend.

At Ellie's house, Josh got out of the limousine and gasped at the sight of his friend in her beautiful, long, blue dress. She smiled and blinked back tears. Three years of fighting bulimia and counting. Josh could see the pain, hidden behind her flawless make-up and slight yet shapely figure. Another item to add to the list of things that must not be allowed to ruin what might be their last night out together, forever.

Josh waited for Ellie to settle into her seat and sat next to her. He could feel George watching him. The finality of the occasion threatened to overwhelm him, and he waited until George's attention had shifted before glancing his way.

George. His best friend. The boy with the bubble of blonde hair, the little ruffian with the rusty bike.

George. The tall, handsome eighteen-year-old, star footballer with his own horse.

George.

Lifting the champagne flute to his lips, George tilted his head back to take some of the fizzy golden liquid into his mouth. He met Josh's gaze, swallowed and smiled. A concerned smile. Josh smiled back. Suddenly, the enormous car was too small, the cooled air was too warm, George was too close, too…beautiful. How had he never noticed before?

The limousine slowed to take on more passengers—Adele, Dan, Andy, Jess—and stopped outside the hotel venue.

"Josh?"

He turned to Ellie, realising they were the only two left in the car.

"Are you all right?"

"Champagne on an empty stomach," he lied and quickly scrambled out, smoothing his jacket, clutching at his scarf. The moment had passed, leaving an invisible, indelible mark.

Around the edges of the ballroom were fifteen round tables, each with ten chairs, a horizontal Ferris wheel swirling burgundy and white and silver. Balloons flittered apart, bumped together, subjects of the draughts and the movements of the sixth formers, a wondrous mass of pastel hues, silver, black and midnight blue, floating above the dance floor.

"Here."

A cold glass was pressed into his hand, and the surreality vanished like a genie returning to its lamp. Josh's eyes found focus again and homed in on George. *Back to normal. Thank goodness.*

"What's up?"

"I don't know. Low blood sugar? I forgot to eat."

George reached into his pocket. "How do you forget to eat?" He pulled out a packet of Polo mints and offered them to Josh.

"Thank you." Josh took two of the mints and passed the packet back. "I don't want this goodbye."

"What do you mean?"

"Tonight." Josh gestured to the banner hanging at the far end of the ballroom, adorned with the words that had haunted him throughout the day. *The end of an era.*

"Ah. You'll soon forget about school when you start uni."

Josh was doubtful. "Do you think that's all it is?"

"Yeah, I do."

***

They were seated for their meal—asparagus soup, roast chicken and seasonal vegetables, chocolate fudge cake and ice cream. A brief awards ceremony followed—Josh, Jess and Ellie received academic accolades, and George and Dan received sports accolades. As soon as the awards were over, Ellie fled, and Josh's heart sank.

"She needs professional help," George whispered.

Josh nodded. A few years from now, he might be in position to offer it. In the meantime, he and George were powerless to do anything more than be her friends and keep her secret. Their mutual helplessness pinned them to their seats while all around them people were rising, music was playing, and the dancing began.

Eventually, George sighed and said, "I'm gonna go and get some more drinks." He set off for the bar.

Josh was so lost in thought about Ellie that it took a moment for George's words to register. "Hold on. I'll give you the money." George waved him away.

"Were you going to leave our table unattended?" Ellie asked, resuming her seat as if nothing was amiss.

"They're allocated seats."

"That doesn't mean they're safe."

"Ellie…"

"Joshua?"

"Will you…" *go to the doctor? Please?* "Stop worrying."

She offered him a feeble smile. "We need to make sure there's always someone at our table. Where are they all?"

Josh glanced around the room. Dan and Andy were standing with the rest of the sporty lads, Jess was talking to a boy, Adele was hanging around the bitchy girls, and Kris was waiting at the bar. George was on his way back with a tray of drinks.

"He's going to drop those," Ellie said.

Josh was already on his feet and moving to intercept. "See, if you hadn't kicked up an unnecessary fuss about us losing our seats, I'd have already been helping him." As he turned George's way, George stumbled, and the glasses slid across the tray. Josh made to grab them, but it was too late. A glass toppled over the edge of the tray, tipping its entire contents—a pint of cider and blackcurrant—all over Josh. He froze and stared down in horror at the huge purple stain forming on his jacket and trousers. His own drink.

"Shit," George hissed. "Sorry."

Josh slowly lifted his head and looked up at George's reddened face. He had his eyes screwed tightly shut, as if blocking the vision would somehow make it unhappen. In an instant, Josh's fury evaporated. He wanted to laugh. He wanted to cry. He wanted...to...

He couldn't look away, and any second George would open his eyes and he would know. He would know of Josh's duplicity. What of their pact, best friends that boyfriends would not tear asunder? No, these feelings could not be, or else—

George opened his eyes, and for a split second, a frown started to form but was quickly replaced by a smile. Still, Josh could not look away. His stomach cramped and then erupted, a fluttering sensation that he knew was his nervous system activated by adrenaline. *Butterflies.* They had paralysed him, left him defenceless, trapped by the emerald gems that sparked and sparkled anew, as if he were seeing George for the first time.

The end of an era.

He could not let these feelings destroy their friendship.

***

Come with me to say goodbye to Maggy.

They were going to different universities, three hundred miles apart, and since the sixth-form ball, Josh had been *weaning* himself off George.

"You'll make loads of new friends," Jess asserted again as if she could tell exactly what he was thinking, even though she wasn't looking his way. She turned around and handed him a pile of A' Level textbooks. "You'll have to."

Silently, he took the books from her and carried them over to the box marked 'charity shop'.

"It's not like George won't make new friends, is it?"

Her words were glass shards of a truth he refused to acknowledge.

Come with me to say goodbye to Maggy.

Josh dropped the books, leaving them in a higgledy-piggledy, pages-splayed heap. "I'll see you later," he said, and left.

***

"I have known you since I was eight." Josh kept his eyes on the Love Heart sweet that was starting to stick to his sweaty palm.

"Seven."

"No. Eight."

"Seven," George insisted. "I was just turned eight when I came to your school, so you were seven."

Josh huffed to hide his frustration, the moment lost. He went for a slight change of approach. "All right. I have known you since *I* was seven, and you've never told me who was your *first love*."

George didn't answer straight away. He was too busy stroking Maggy. "It's…" he began. "I, err…"

"Sorry." Josh hadn't meant to embarrass him.

"It's OK."

"I should've just gone for a horse-it."

George smiled nervously, seemingly relieved to be let off the hook, and Josh assumed the answer was Kris. Why wouldn't it be?

A few turns later, the same phrase came up again. This time he didn't hesitate in passing it off as a forfeit. His hand shook as he held it out to Maggy, the tiny round sweet in the middle of his palm, his only chance to say something before he left for university, eaten by a horse.

Be mine.

My boy.

Kiss me.

It's true.

George forfeited every single one. When the game was all but over, he placed a purple sweet, face down, in Josh's hand.

Josh accepted it with a sad smile. "The purple ones always were my favourites."

"Don't eat it," George said quickly.

Josh flipped the sweet over. The words blurred as his eyes filled with tears. *For keeps.*

"I promised, didn't I?" George asked. Josh sniffed and rubbed at his nose. "Whatever happens, our friendship is for keeps."

Josh nodded, not trusting himself to speak. He put the sweet in his pocket and held out his little finger. George's little finger hooked with his.

***

George had gone. Left for Aberdeen that morning. Three months since their sixth-form ball, and those feelings had not diminished in the slightest. Josh loved George. He'd always loved George, but not like this. He was losing sleep, and his waking mind was clouded by daydreams, dark and destructive, *cumulonimbus.* The storm must not break.

Their days of cycling were over, but their friendship might survive. Josh took the lock from his pocket, the heavy, brass padlock that had kept their bikes safe. He fastened it to the chain and tucked it away, above the ledge under the road, and returned to the canal bank. He looked back at the concrete slope, their haven on hot summer days, so many perfect memories. The padlock would keep those safe too.

With his hand clasped around the key, Josh turned and slowly walked away, wondering if he would ever visit the viaduct again.

George
(aged 26)

W HEN GEORGE HAD received the call from the livery stables about Maggy, it had changed his life. Something had spooked her, and she'd tried to jump the paddock fence, critically injuring her spine. There was nothing anyone could do, and they'd offered to keep her comfortable until he could get home from uni to say goodbye, but he couldn't bear the thought of her suffering, and in any case, he'd wanted to remember the affectionate, fun-loving young horse, not a crippled animal waiting to be put out of her misery. The stables handled the arrangements with the vet and assured George that someone would be with Maggy right to the end.

Maggy had not been the reason George had chosen a degree in agricultural studies, although her death was the reason he'd avoided working with animals in the five years since he'd graduated. He'd gone home the weekend after her accident, and Josh had also travelled back from uni, so they could say goodbye in their own way. She had been only three years old, and George had spent so little time with her it shouldn't have hurt the way it did. The only consolation had been having Josh's arms around him while they fed an entire packet of Love Hearts to the horses and ponies in the paddock.

Those few hours of comfort had kept George going for months after. He had missed Josh so much and lived for the summer and Christmas breaks, when they both came home and spent time together, sometimes with their other friends but usually just the two of them. They didn't cycle together anymore, but they still went for long walks, and they could talk for hours, even though phoning and writing to each other as often as they did meant there was very little left to say.

There was, however, one thing that George had never said. Three years apart as undergraduates, after which George came home whilst Josh stayed at uni to complete his Master's degree, and still George didn't know how to tell him. Because that urge he had first felt under the viaduct when he was thirteen hadn't gone away. If anything, it became stronger each time they saw each other, and he decided. When Josh finally came home for good, if George still felt the same way, he'd tell him.

I'm in love with you.

***

George sidestepped between the customers standing three-deep at the bar, trying to work his way to the beer garden at the back of the pub. He'd never been here before, as it was local to Kris and Shaunna's new house. It was only when he stepped out of the door and into the fresh evening air that he realised he'd been holding his breath. He scanned the crowded beer garden and spotted Kris, sitting at a table in the corner. He was reading a book but must have sensed George's arrival; he closed the book, looked up and smiled.

"Hi." Kris edged around the table to hug him.

"Hi. How are you doing?"

"Great. We've been working on the house all day. Hanging wallpaper." Kris released George and held up his hands, showing off his scraped knuckles. George winced on Kris's behalf. "It's looking good, though. Just our bedroom to do now and we're finished."

"Awesome." George attempted a smile, but it proved too much.

"I bought you a pint of lager. I hope that's OK."

"Perfect." George took a long swig, swallowed and looked around him. "Busy, isn't it?"

"Do you want to go somewhere quieter?"

George considered it, but between the music and the multiple conversations, it was unlikely anyone would hear what they were talking about. He shook his head. "Here's fine."

Now all he had to do was talk, because if he didn't tell someone, he would go fully out of his mind. He sipped at his drink, a slow, steady motion at odds with the churning mess inside his head as the events of the past few months tumbled around his brain, colliding, mixing, muddying his thoughts.

"Has something happened?" Kris asked.

George laughed sadly. "Yeah. Lots of things." He put his drink down but kept hold of the glass, focusing on the bubbles rising to the surface and wishing his words would do the same. He briefly glanced up and met Kris's concerned gaze, but he couldn't hold it. "My dad died."

"Oh, George. I'm sorry."

"Thanks." He closed his eyes, shook his head. "I haven't seen him in eighteen years. Not since he walked out on us. I was never sure if my mum kicked him out. Either way, it doesn't matter. He made a new life for himself in Colorado."

"How did you find out he'd died?"

"His lawyer sent a fax to a lawyer in town, and they forwarded it on." George sat back and ran his hands over his head. He should have been elated, but he wasn't. He was disappointed. "Dad left his estate to me."

Kris's eyebrows rose. "Did he have anything worth leaving?"

"Yep. A ranch."

"A ranch? Like with cattle and horses and all that jazz?"

George nodded. "Do you remember the horse I had before uni?"

"Vaguely."

"That was my eighteenth birthday present from my dad. He sent me a card to say he'd bought her. He set her up in livery, paid for riding lessons, vet bills—everything other than contact me directly."

"He was expecting you to call him."

"Exactly, and I wasn't gonna do that. I can't forgive him for abandoning us, not even knowing he's dead. And the ranch means nothing."

"Presumably you're going to sell it?"

George let his hands fall to his lap. "Well, here's the thing. I'm…" He took a deep breath and said it quickly. "I'm in love with Josh."

Kris nodded once. "Tell me something I don't know."

"Err…" George had expected Kris to be surprised by his admission. "Did Josh say something?"

"God, no. I don't think we've actually had one proper conversation since he got back from uni. When was that? Two years ago? It's…I'm not sure. Like he's hugging us all at arm's length, if you see what I mean?"

"Yeah, unfortunately." The distance Josh had put between them was the reason George was here now, pouring out his soul to Kris. "How did you know? About my feelings for Josh."

"OK…" A few times, Kris took a breath as if he was about to speak, but then he looked away. Whatever he was preparing to say, George got the impression he wasn't going to like it. Kris turned to face him again and made firm eye contact. "George, I love you—as a friend. I need you to understand that before I go any further."

George still wasn't sure where Kris was going, but he accepted the statement as truth. "I love you too."

"And I've always loved you, but I also knew I couldn't compete."

"What do you mean?"

"With Josh."

"You're talking about when you and I were together?"

"Yeah, and you're probably going to tell me you weren't in love with him then. I'm not necessarily saying you were, but whatever the bond is between the two of you, no-one else stands a chance."

"He's not in love with me."

"He told you that?"

George sighed deeply. "No. He didn't say anything."

"What happened?"

George wasn't sure he wanted to share the full, humiliating tale of the night he and Josh had gone to cinema. He hadn't planned to tell Josh, not that night, but it fell out of his mouth. *I think I love you. No, I don't. I know. I always have.* They'd been standing in the queue, waiting to buy popcorn, and the woman behind the counter had raised her voice to get their attention. Josh had mumbled incoherently, George had asked him what he'd said, and he'd replied, "Nothing."

That was months ago, and only Ellie was aware of what had happened. George had come clean, as Ellie's wedding was the weekend after their cinema trip, and he couldn't bear the thought of seeing Josh, trying to pretend everything was all right when it wasn't. Eighteen years of friendship straight down the pan. He wished he'd kept his mouth shut. Desperately wished…

No, that wasn't true. He wished he'd said something sooner. On the night of the sixth-form ball, when it had hit him like a punch in the gut. The urge to kiss Josh that he'd fought to keep at bay had been growing inside him the whole time, and it had somehow broken free, perhaps fuelled by Josh's sudden vulnerability when the drinks had spilled over him. Or the glint in his eyes that George thought he'd seen—was convinced of it, or he had been back then.

How often he'd wondered whether telling Josh would have made any difference, because whatever happened to him at university, it had turned him into someone else. Gone was the innocent, perpetually inquisitive boy whose honesty could compliment or equally offend. The spark of imagined mischief that had lit up his azure eyes had been entirely snuffed out. No more smiles or giggles or puzzled frowns. Just a robot Josh, his spirit broken.

Broken.

But he'd been getting better. After two years of George calling him and asking if he could visit only to be fended off with constant excuses of assignment deadlines and too much research,

Josh had come home from uni and bought his own place. He needed privacy, he'd said, and George could understand that. George had shared a house with other students, and they'd all got along great, but nothing was sacred. Guaranteed any time he was in the shower, one of them would need to use the toilet, and they'd walk right in and do so. If one of them needed a clean pair of socks, they'd think nothing of nicking them off someone else, and whatever food and alcohol was in the kitchen belonged to everybody.

George didn't suppose all uni houses were like that, but he could imagine how hard it would have been for Josh to share with other people, even if they'd had clearer house rules than the musketeer mentality that had existed up in Aberdeen. It was all speculation on George's part; Josh had never mentioned his housemates—he rarely talked about life at uni at all—but he *had* been getting better, gradually allowing George close again. It would have been enough, but George had to ask for more, and now *they* were broken; irreparably, permanently broken, and robot Josh was back.

He still sounded the same. He talked the way he always had about the people around him, the world at large. He was as sarcastic and funny as ever...if George ignored the feeling of loss. *His* Josh had asked 'will we always be best friends?' *This* Josh spoke only of friendship as a general connection that could happen with anyone, although he'd admitted that their friendship group was more important to him than life itself. The words were enormous, yet their delivery was so ordinary, like 'my favourite meal is...', and hearing them made George want to fall to his knees and bang his fists on the ground. *I want my best friend back. Please, I want him back.*

"I asked him if he'd come with me," George said.

"To Colorado?"

"I've got nothing to lose." He shrugged. "It's tearing me apart."

Kris smiled in sympathy. "What did he say?"

"Nothing. I asked him in a letter, and he didn't reply."

"Maybe he didn't get it?"

"Oh, he got it, all right. Now he's not talking to me at all—as if things weren't awkward enough before. I wrecked our friendship, Kris, and I can't stay here. I can't keep waiting for his answer, but God, I don't want to leave. I wish…" George swallowed back the lump in his throat. "Which means your house-warming will be the last time we're all together. Sorry." George put his head down, squeezing his eyes shut, fighting to keep the tears from spilling. Kris's hand closed around his.

"He loves you, George," he said. George shook his head. "He does. You've waited a long time for him, and honestly? I think he might keep you waiting forever. Until he accepts who he is—"

George looked up, not angry, pleading. He was at the end of his tether. "Please, don't start lecturing about coming out."

Kris smiled gently. "I'm not. You deserve to be happy. That's all I'm saying. And I don't want you to leave either. But…I think you've made the right decision."

"Thanks. What else can I do?"

***

If George had ever possessed any pretence of being the sort of man who didn't cry, it was well and truly lost by the time his plane was boarding. He commanded himself not to look back, yet as soon as his boarding pass had been checked and returned to him, he couldn't help it. Beyond the partition were eight of the nine most important people in his life; he and his mum had said their goodbyes at home—*just me and this little bastard to feed now, then*. At least he'd been smiling while he sobbed. Now he was even past sobbing.

With one final wave, George turned away from his friends and stepped into the tunnel that led to the plane. It was like walking towards the light and knowing he couldn't fight it any longer. This was his only chance at finding…not happiness, but peace of mind.

George reached his seat and settled into it with seat belt fastened and eyes shut. It was the closest he could get to being alone with the pictures of Josh in his mind—not the shell of a man who had solemnly embraced him and waved goodbye as if they would see each other tomorrow, but the little sandy-haired boy with beautiful blue eyes and lashes so blonde that George had to look hard to see them.

Why are you staring?

I'm looking for your eyelashes.

They're above and below my eyes.

They've gone.

You're silly, George.

The memory still made him smile. And if his memory should ever fail him, he had photos—from school, and their sixth-form ball, and the day Josh was awarded his Master's in Counselling and Psychotherapy. They were standing back-to-back, and as the photo was about to be taken, Josh had taken off his mortar-board hat and put it on George. They'd both been laughing so much they'd ended up with stitch, but were it not for that photograph, George would have forgotten, because Josh had already changed by that time. The day of the ceremony was a temporary flashback to good times, bike rides, video games and too many sweets.

Looking back, it seemed almost as if Josh had been making a point, trying to prove he was happy. Whether it was to himself or to George or the rest of the world might forever remain a mystery. Just like his lack of response to George's confession that he loved—no—he was *in love with* Josh. And until Josh offered evidence to the contrary, George would hold on to that one tiny thread of hope. That maybe Josh was in love with him too.

Josh
(mid-thirties)

"HELLO?"

"Hey, George, it's Josh." He said it as if the call was an everyday occurrence, rather than the first time he had initiated contact since George had left the country.

"Hey, yourself! What on earth are you doing calling me at—must be four in the morning?"

"Yes, about that." Josh slowly vented a sigh of relief. *Same old George, skirting around the crux of the matter. What on earth am I doing calling you after ten years of ignoring your every attempt at communicating with me?* "How are you?"

"I'm great. I sent you an email this morning. Did you get it?"

"I did, thanks." He'd received it, read it, committed it to memory. He could recall every word of every email and every letter George had ever sent him, but not once had he replied. How could he, when the only thing he had to say was the one thing he could not?

"Yep. So," George said, breaking the silence. "What's up, then? You not sleeping too well, I guess?"

"I'm sleeping OK, other than I keep having this dream. I've lost count of how many times."

That was only part of the story; the rest was likely the reason he was having the same dream over and over again. When Josh had said his friends were more important to him than life itself, it had not been an overstatement, and as soon as it looked like their friendship group was falling apart, Josh had turned to the only person he knew could help him. The only one he trusted.

He could probably have cut straight to the chase, but he didn't want the call to end. Not yet. So he recounted his dream, in detail, and it was all rather mundane. It involved him being naked and either falling or being pushed into a giant tubular blue waterslide. Not really the stuff of nightmares…so long as he ignored the symbolism.

When Josh was done, George stayed quiet for a moment as if pondering the meaning of the dream, although Josh was fairly sure that wasn't what he was doing. More likely he was weighing up the wisdom of a witty retort, because eventually he came back with, "Well, you're the therapist."

"That's exactly what Ellie said."

"What I mean is, I can't say what it might mean."

"I didn't tell you so you could interpret it for me, George."

"You called me because no-one else is up, didn't you?"

"No. Not at all. At least, no-one else is up, but I saw your email, and I thought I should give you a call. I did always like being your friend, you know. Nowadays we don't seem to get the chance to talk. Not like we used to."

"Nowadays? Ten years…"

"Don't blame me!" Josh complained defensively.

"How about you just try answering my emails occasionally? I know it must be hard for you…"

"I don't respond because I don't want to give you the wrong idea."

"Ah, man, not that again. I got my head around it a long time ago. I can't change how I feel about you, but I do accept you don't feel the same, and I'm fine with that. Really."

There was a very long pause, for a telephone conversation, at least. Josh chewed on his lip as he considered what George had said. It was an age since they properly, honestly talked to each other, and he'd missed it more than he wanted to admit. George accepted they were just friends; surely he could do the same?

"Ten years, huh?" *Almost.* It was actually nine years, eleven months, three weeks, four days…

∗∗∗

Josh had arrived at the airport far too early, even for him. He'd checked the arrivals board, drunk coffee, checked the arrivals board, read a book, checked the arrivals board, drunk more coffee... Now, as the flow of passengers began to slow, he tried not to fidget, watching, watching, until at last, George emerged, grinning from ear to ear and wearing a cowboy hat. He put away his boarding pass and passport and walked towards Josh, who found himself moving forward without any conscious effort.

"Man, it's good to see you." George threw his arms around him and squeezed tight.

"You too," Josh replied, not releasing his grip for a moment. He could hardly believe George was here. Admittedly, he'd visited home plenty of times during the past ten years, and they'd even gone over—as a whole group—to Colorado to see him twice. But this time, it was profoundly different. Josh had been the reason George had left, and therefore only he could be the reason George returned. One phone call was all it had taken. Just one call to say *I need you.*

***

That phone call two years ago had merely been a stepping stone. After eighteen years of hiding the truth behind friendship, his job and his need for solitude, Josh still clung to his mask, knowing that one day it would slip away, beyond his grasp. He had tried to forget—not George. How could he ever forget George? But he'd done everything he could to cast out those feelings because they weren't real. At school, sixth form, university, he saw it all around him. Lust, infatuation, crushes, love—so many labels stuck over the same underlying process: interpersonal attraction, intimacy and desire.

Without desire, his love for George was a phantom entity, a manifestation of Josh's desperation to be like everyone else. His 'gift', which for so long set him apart from his peers, had also offered him a gateway to their world. He had learned how to make friends much as he had learned the intricacies of the English language and the theories and concepts of his academic discipline—through observation, research and the tutelage of others. He had even learned to accept that his experience of the world was not only different, it was also uniquely painful and would always be so. But the one thing he could not learn—for it came from within, not without—was desire.

The tutelage of others. In reality, there had been just one other who had come close to filling George's shoes. *Close, but no cigar.* Sean was an impoverished Irish student who had arrived at university three days after everyone else. He had been Josh's classmate, his halls mate, and ultimately his housemate. Sean was proud, like George, and fought Josh all the way, rejecting his handouts, accepting his quirks. He had shown Josh how humility could mediate the devastation wreaked by his gift, and for a time, he had been the best friend Josh had. He would forever be the only one who could have saved his life.

Josh curled his fingers, trying to make fists of his useless hands. Perhaps one day he would feel genuine gratitude for what Sean had done. It all depended on what happened now he had revisited the viaduct and unlocked the past.

With the vanity case once more safely stowed in the loft, he paused, listening for any signs of life... *Nothing.* He shuffled the hatch closed, quietly returned downstairs and out to the shed, to put the ladders back, carefully stepping over the suitcases.

Suitcases.

Josh had noticed them some time ago, and at first he'd thought little of it. After George had sold the ranch and returned to England, he'd been left with enough money to pay rent and not much else. Finding full-time work proved impossible, and he'd gone back to college. The house he'd rented had been in a terrible state of disrepair, he was broke, and in any case, their friendship was as strong as it had been when they were at school. So they'd reached an agreement. In return for George doing the shopping—which Josh hated—and cooking their meals—

which Josh also hated—George would share Josh's house rent-free until such point as he finished his course or found a job.

Given George's perpetual resistance to being a 'charity case', his eagerness to also mow the lawn or change blown light bulbs or undertake any task that, coincidentally, required a trip to the garden shed did not seem in the least bit suspicious. And it was by accident rather than design that every time Josh went out to the shed, he was home alone. Or, rather, it was intentional in the sense that he'd still not shaken his fear of heights and didn't want to rely on George's assistance.

But he wasn't hiding the fact he knew George's suitcases were in the shed because it hadn't occurred to him that George *might be hiding them* until two weeks ago, when he'd claimed he didn't know where they were. He'd even gone through the pantomime of searching the house for them, and Josh had played along with it, all the while fighting to contain the joyous relief flooding his body and mind with warmth and peace. He wasn't the only one keeping secrets.

He should have been ashamed of himself, but desperation overrode everything. He needed to know George's secrets, to know if they were the same as his, so he went snooping. What he found was the key to the lock on his heart. *George still loved him.* Not that Josh had ever doubted it, but rebuilding their friendship had relied on putting the past behind him, just as George had.

I accept you don't feel the same, and I'm fine with that.

In Josh's defence, it was only *preliminary* snooping. He'd looked through George's photos, but he'd left the rest of his possessions untouched. The knowledge that George had hoarded the mementos of their life, together and apart, was enough. Josh had removed the lock from his ottoman. Now all he had to do was wait for his own hoard of mementos to be discovered.

A few hours later, after George had gone out for the day, Josh brought George's suitcase of photos into the house and stood it in the hallway. He had new wallpaper to hang in the living room and decided it would be the perfect excuse for how he had 'suddenly stumbled across' George's stuff in the shed.

George arrived home...with a new suitcase. He stopped dead, his eyes widening at the sight of his old suitcase. "Oh. You found it."

"Yes. It was in the shed, along with three others."

"What were you doing in the shed?"

"Looking for a paste brush. More to the point, what were *they* doing in the shed? Any idea?"

"I, err, well I guess I must've put them there."

"And you didn't happen to notice them, right in front of the lawn mower, you know, the last time you mowed the grass? Now when was that? Last weekend?"

George was avoiding Josh's probing gaze. If he could make George look up, it could be over right now, but no. George kept his eyes on the suitcase. "I'll take it upstairs, shall I?" he suggested. He reached for the handle. Josh put out his foot and stopped him.

"Not so fast, Morley. What's inside?"

"Nothing important. In fact, so unimportant I can't remember exactly what. Old documents. That sort of thing?"

He briefly glanced at Josh. A nervous smile flickered across his face. *Not today.* Josh moved his foot out of the way and stepped aside. George stayed where he was.

"Off you go, then." Josh turned towards the living room. "And when you're done you can come and give me a hand with this last wall."

It was disheartening to say the least, and every other hint Josh offered that evening—telling George he was happy they were sharing a house, and that their friendship was back to how it used to be, and that they should *go and see a movie together sometime*—went unacknowledged.

The next day, George left the house first thing and stayed out until late, and again the day after. There was no denying that he was avoiding Josh, and he would have kept doing so indefinitely were it not for an impromptu sixth-form reunion, seemingly thrown together on a whim by one of their old school friends, with the ludicrous requirement that they wear their original outfits. Serendipity's work, perhaps?

It was twenty years since their sixth-form ball. Josh's suit was still in its bag at the back of the wardrobe. His hands were shaking as he unzipped the bag, setting more memories free.

"Mine went back to the charity shop," George said as Josh flew past on his way out to the dry cleaner's.

"That must be disappointing for you."

"Oh, yeah." George made a sad face.

Josh rolled his eyes. "If you need a loan—"

"It's in hand, thanks."

Sure enough, on Saturday night, George was wearing another new-old suit, but this one fitted him without the need for last-minute alterations.

"Have you seen a…ah!" Josh pulled the pink silk scarf free of the sofa cushion. He draped it around his neck and turned to George. "OK. I'm ready, and with five minutes to spare. How impressive is that? *And* the dry cleaner got rid of that blackcurrant stain—not bad after twenty years, huh?" He pointed at his pristine trousers to emphasise the point and smiled.

George didn't respond, didn't move, didn't look away, as if he were in some kind of trance.

"What's the matter?" Josh examined the front of his shirt. "Don't tell me I've spilt something down me already."

"No, you haven't. You look… You look kind of like Don Johnson, only… You look very dapper."

"Thanks." Josh was still trying to ignore George's odd behaviour. "So do you, although how is it that you've reached our age without being able to fasten a tie properly?"

"Well, on the ranch we found they kind of got in the way of herding and clearing out stables and stuff," he said as Josh approached him. "And they don't go well with T-shirts."

George's heart was beating so hard and fast that Josh felt it against the side of his hand. He placed his palm on George's chest. "Are you feeling OK?"

"Yeah. Why?"

"Your heart's racing. Excited about tonight? It's going to be great fun."

"I hope so."

"There you go." Josh smiled and gave the tie a final tug to straighten it just as Kris knocked on the door. George's relief at having a reason to get away from him was tangible.

It only got worse from there. Jess and Adele had a horrendous argument in the limousine, and George got caught in the crossfire. Without thinking, Josh grabbed George's hand to comfort him. He felt George tense, but now he'd done it, he couldn't let go. It was a reunion, a rerun of the original night. It was the perfect time to tell George the truth. But he was already acting so strangely, and what if it destroyed their friendship all over again?

It was better not to say anything at all than to risk losing everything. Better to enjoy an evening out with friends, keep a housemate, keep their secrets safely locked away.

Better not to see George and Kris, together.

So much for unlocking his heart.

∗

Four days had passed since the night of the reunion. Four days of going through the motions of getting up, going to work, trying not to scream at George and wishing he would leave. He wasn't angry with George. He was angry with himself for still craving what everyone else had. Watching George at the reunion, no longer hiding away...Josh was so proud of him. If only he could disentangle that feeling from the mess of envy, love, hopelessness... But George didn't understand any of that. From his perspective, Josh was angry with him, and he wanted to know why. He'd even confessed, hoping it would clear the air.

*

"Hey, I'm really, really sorry about Saturday."

"What about Saturday?"

"Me and Kris. I mean, it wasn't—"

"That's not what this is about!"

"It isn't? Ellie told me you saw us together, and I thought—"

"Whatever you thought, or she thought, you're both wrong. You and Kris, well, you've always been like that."

"Not since we were at school, which was the only reason we ended up…doing that on Saturday."

"That's just it. The only difference between Saturday and any other time is that you and he kissed. What I'm talking about is the underlying desire to take it further."

George shook his head. His eyes were blazing with fury. "So it's because you think we want to screw each other? What the hell difference does it make to you if we do?"

"None, really."

"Well that's just great, isn't it? D'you know, I think I might go and stay with my mum for a few days."

"As you like. If you'd rather sleep on a couch than sort this out, then that's entirely up to you."

"No. I wouldn't, but if you won't talk to me, I don't see I have much choice, really. And for the record, I do not want to have sex with Kris. Not then, not now, not ever."

*

Josh had wanted to call George, but he had no idea what to say. Sorry would be a good place to start. He was punishing George for his own failings, *and* he'd been through his email. But then, George had snooped in Josh's ottoman, and he felt violated. It was absurd. He'd intentionally removed the lock, hoping for exactly that to happen. Now it had happened.

It had happened.

Josh was ready. There would be no more games. He went to get his phone from upstairs, typing the text message on his way back down.

When are you coming home? I miss you.

He sent it and put his phone in his pocket, took it out again, typed a second message, read it back and pressed 'send' before he lost his nerve.

***

George heard his phone beeping in the distance, although he knew it wasn't actually in the distance, because he was in that half-asleep, half-awake state where dreams merge in and out of reality. He rolled over and stretched, the sensation of another person in the bed proving to be the most effective alarm clock in the world. Not his mum. One night on her lumpy couch was one night too many. And not Kris, either, because there was nothing going on. There was only one person George wanted to be with, and if that couldn't be, he'd stay single forever.

"Morning," Shaunna yawned, flicking her hair out of her face and straight into his.

"Good morning," he replied.

Shaunna spun her legs off the bed and sat up. "Cup of tea in bed, or is that a step too far into weird?"

"No. That'd be lovely, thanks," he said, reaching over for his phone. He read the message and was about to lock the screen as another one came through. He scrolled, read the second message and threw his phone down on top of the duvet. Then he sat up and read it again.

"Bad news?" Shaunna asked.

"I am definitely awake, aren't I?" She nodded. "This isn't a dream?" She shook her head. "Read this." He passed her the phone. She shook her head again and passed it back to him. He reactivated the dimmed screen and gave it to her once more.

"You still want that tea?"

"No. I'm good for tea, thanks."

George had the quickest shower he'd ever had, scrubbed manically at his teeth, decided to forego the shave, and cleared the stairs in three bounds.

"I'll see you later," he called on his way out.

***

Cutting diagonally across the road, George slowed his pace as he neared the house. He hesitated. This was entirely new ground, and he wasn't sure how to act. Should he pretend everything was the same as it had always been? Should he knock, or just let himself in? He paused at the gate to give himself thinking time, and to prepare for the possibility that the message was some kind of hoax or misunderstanding.

"Are you going to stand there all day?"

He glanced up to find Josh leaning against the doorpost, looking the way he always had, yet somehow very different. And then it came to him in a flurry of realisation. He had dropped his guard.

Walking up that path was the strangest experience, and he imagined it to be how a moth would feel if it developed a level of self-awareness which allowed it to reason. Irrespective of how attractive that bright, shiny object appeared to be, it probably wasn't the moon; but it *might* be, and it was worth risking everything for that small, impossible chance.

Josh watched him, a gleam of impatience—*or is it eagerness?*— in his eyes, willing him inside, into the trap.

"I'm scared," George said.

"Me too." Josh moved to allow him to pass in close proximity, but then blocked him with his arm. "I'm so scared, George. I don't know if I can do this, but I've got to try. I can't lose you."

"You're not going to lose me. Don't you understand that yet?"

George
(mid-thirties)

GEORGE HAD FINISHED reading the letters Josh had written to him and never sent—declarations that he missed him, thought about him constantly, and loved him. There were secrets, too, that Josh was sharing for the first time, of how he had never felt sexual desire, his confusion over his feelings and his sorrow that they could never be together. All George took from it was *he loves me*.

His suitcase lay open on the floor, spilling over with hundreds of snapshots, bent and tattered from being tossed about in the backs of trucks or dumped uncaringly in cargo holds, jumbled and no longer in any discernible order. Josh had confessed to having already looked through George's photos, and George had owned up to doing the same, although he'd gone no further than that. There were dangerous secrets in Josh's past; George saw how he struggled to keep them hidden, locked safely away, and when the time came, they would face those secrets together.

They'd shared photos and letters—George had even shared his sketchbook, or the one he still had in his possession. His first, bought for his O' Level course, had long been lost. It was crazy to think how worried he'd been about it getting into the wrong hands—for Josh or anyone else to have seen the rudimentary sketches of a teenaged boy in love with his best friend. George smiled at the memory of those innocent times before he'd told Josh he was in love with him. Today, for the first time, he knew he had done the right thing.

Josh reached the end of George's letters—the ones *he* had written and never sent—but returned to the first one and started reading it again.

"I'm going to make coffee," George said.

"I'll come with you."

"Are you serious?"

"Yes, George, I am completely serious. I think we've wasted enough time, and right now I want to spend every minute with you."

"OK. If you say so."

Well this is new. Josh being clingy and affectionate? George carried the cups to the kitchen, with Josh following closely behind, still engrossed in the letters.

"This bit with the horse whisperer? It's the only time you actually sounded like you were enjoying yourself."

"Yeah. It was amazing. I didn't realise how easy it was to tune in to animals or get them to tune in to you. Horses are really responsive like that. You kind of get into this zone where suddenly you know exactly how they feel and what they're going to do next. The first time I did it was so weird, like magic, although it's really only about correctly interpreting their posture and movement."

"Body language—same as with people," Josh said. He was watching George closely, reading *his* body language. It made him feel very self-conscious.

"Tell me about that spark," George said, both to shift the attention away from himself, and because he wanted to hear what that first moment had been like for Josh.

"You already know. You just read it."

"Tell me anyway."

Josh sighed and closed his eyes. He was thinking, remembering, countless expressions flitting across his face like clouds over the moon—a smile, a frown, a grimace, another smile...

"OK," he said, still with eyes closed. "This is how I remember it. You were buying a round of drinks, and I was sitting at the table with Ellie. She was getting worked up over us losing our chairs, even though we had allocated seats from the sit-down meal. You brought the drinks on a tray and nearly tripped with it. I got up to help, but it was too late. My drink slid right off the tray and all over me. You blushed and screwed your eyes tight shut. When you opened them again, you realised I was staring at you. You smiled, and I couldn't look away. It was like you'd changed into someone new, right there before me, and I couldn't take my eyes off you. It made me feel dizzy, sick—I'm getting the same butterflies now just thinking about it."

All the while Josh had been telling the story, in his head, George had been repeating *no way, no way...* Josh opened his eyes and smiled bashfully. George shook his head. "No way!"

"You don't believe me?"

"Yes, I believe you. Just...wow, man. That's..." He was still reeling in shock and amazement.

"What about you?" Josh asked. "When did you know? And don't say 'from the moment we met'. We were in junior school."

"You can't be in love when you're eight?"

"Seven."

"I was eight," George argued.

"You're deflecting."

"Yep." George grinned.

Josh rolled his eyes. "George!"

"OK...well..." He began slowly, pausing for dramatic effect. Josh shot him a glare, and he picked up his speed. "It was also at the sixth-form ball. I was buying us a round of drinks, and you were sitting at our table with Ellie. I think she might have been stressing about us losing our chairs, and I'd been to the bar... need I go on?"

"No way!" Josh's mouth fell open. "You mean...wow!"

They both laughed and continued to gaze at each other in wonder. After twenty years, they'd finally discovered they fell for one another at the very same moment. What to do about it: that was the question.

"Kettle's boiled," Josh said.

"Yep."

"Best make the coffee."

"Yep." George snapped out of it and poured hot water into the empty mugs. Josh tutted and pushed the coffee jar towards him, their hands touching briefly in transit and making George gasp. It was electric. Josh turned away.

"Is that why you didn't tell me?" George tried to make light of the question, as if it mattered less than the granules of coffee tumbling from the spoon in his shaking hand. "In your letters— the sex thing?" The lack of reply was confirmation in itself. "Josh. Please don't push me away, not now."

"I'm not. It's just…"

"I know. I read your letter. You still feel the same?"

"Which is why we could never make it work. I watched you at the reunion, battling to be yourself in front of all those people. And I was so proud of you, for knowing who and what you are and having the guts to show them."

"You don't know what you are. Is that what you're saying?"

"That's the problem. I don't think I'm anything. I'm not saying I don't get aroused, but obtaining sexual release isn't the same as having a sexual relationship."

"So you've never wanted to…act on it?"

"Once or twice, but in general, no."

George had been stirring the mugs the whole time and was still stirring them now. He stopped and handed one to Josh. "So what's changed? Why tell me all of this now if you're so certain it won't work?"

Josh fell into a deep, thoughtful silence, no flickers of smiles this time, just pain and confusion. *We could never make it work.* If Josh truly believed that, surely he'd have stayed quiet?

"You've been so distant," he said.

"*I've* been distant?" George asked incredulously.

"Yes, I know I have too, but I thought you were leaving me, and it must've flipped a switch in my head. I don't know if you remember Richard—my client with Asperger's Syndrome?"

"Sort of."

"When I told him I'd never been in love, I honestly believed that."

"Hang on." George wanted to check he was getting it right. "So you think being in love means you should also want to have sex?"

Again, the absence of a response gave Josh away.

"Do you realise how ridiculous that is?"

"Is it?"

"Everything we had—friendship, trust, *love*—you dismissed over that one small thing."

"The most important thing."

"No, it's not. The other day, when you accused Kris and me—"

"I didn't accuse you."

"Let me finish, please?"

Josh sipped his coffee by way of assent. George rephrased and continued.

"You said there was always something between Kris and me, that we wanted each other, but it didn't necessarily mean anything."

"It's true. Just because you desire him—"

George shook his head in exasperation. "*I don't.* Obviously, I *did* when we were together. And of course we did stuff together, but we never had sex, not in the way you mean. Kris was my first boyfriend, and I was his, so yes, maybe we do have some kind of hold over each other, but none of that is *being in love*, and it wasn't why he kissed me at the reunion party either. He was trying to prove a point—that no-one would care—and he was wrong."

"Did you love him?"

"Yes. And I still do, as a friend, although sometimes he really pisses me off, especially when he pulls stunts like that. Growing up where I did, you don't go around advertising it, and I know he thinks he's doing it for all the right reasons, but it's a different world."

"Were you ever in love with him?" Josh asked quietly.

"Do you mean that, or are you asking if I ever wanted to have sex with him?"

Josh frowned and started chewing the inside of his cheek.

"No," George replied, for the answer was the same either way. "I've never been in love with anyone but you."

"And what about sex?"

"Well, I wouldn't say no. We've known each other for thirty years, and I've been in love with you for twenty of those. I'd be lying if I told you it had never crossed my mind."

He sensed Josh's anxiety escalating, but there was no point lying about it. George's very first flutterings of desire had accompanied the urge to kiss Josh, and he had imagined— fantasised—what it would be like to make love to him. It was happening more and more, like before the reunion, when Josh fixed his tie for him, he'd wanted to say *hang the party* and push Josh down onto the sofa. Although with what Josh had told him, that kind of thing would likely never happen.

Josh picked up the dishcloth and brushed the spilled coffee granules into his hand.

"But it's not that important," George said quickly. "The way you start cleaning when you're stressing out or hide behind your hair when you don't want me to know how you're feeling? That's the stuff that matters."

"I don't understand."

"Today is the first time we've ever talked about sex. Doesn't that tell you something?"

Josh shrugged and moved towards the sink. George intercepted and disarmed him of the dishcloth.

"Are you listening?" George waited for eye contact. "Good. I'll try to keep this short and simple. You see, there are lots of things I love about you. Your smile, your eyes, the way you snort when you laugh, and how you spend hours messing with your hair for it to end up looking the same as ever. I love that you're intelligent and quick-witted, and that little know-it-all thing you do when someone says something that you think is stupid.

I love your obsession with having everything in the right place, and the look of contentment you get when it's all 'just so'. I love how you try not to offend me when you hate what I've cooked, and how you always put the knives back in the right place when you wash up. I even love—"

"OK! I get the message!" Josh put his finger on George's lips. It was an action that both silenced him and momentarily stopped him breathing. Josh smiled and released him. "Although I still don't see why the paring knife has to be on the left, and the vegetable knife…" George raised an eyebrow. "Anyway, as long as it makes you happy."

"It does," George assured him. "But do you understand what I'm saying?" Josh nodded. "And do you still think being in love means wanting to have sex?"

"No. I guess not."

"What do you think now?"

George was desperate to hear those words, and he could see Josh trying to say them, but he was scared.

"*I miss holding your hand, George. Sometimes it feels like we aren't best friends anymore.*"

"*But we are.*"

"*Do you promise?*"

"I think I'm in love with you, George, but I don't know."

"Because you don't want to have sex with me?"

"No. Yes. How the hell am I supposed to answer that?" Josh blushed and put his head down so that his hair fell over his face.

George laughed and gently lifted Josh's chin with his finger. "You know? Whichever of those it is, I'm OK with it."

Still Josh kept his eyes averted.

"Hey," George prompted. He waited for Josh to look up, brushed the hair back from his face, and whispered, *I promise.*

Epilogue:
Love, Unlocked

Kiss me."
"Really?"
"Really."
"Umm. OK." George leaned forward and planted the quickest, lightest kiss on Josh's lips.
"No. Kiss me properly."
Josh was staring deep into his eyes, and even if he'd wanted to resist, which he didn't, there was absolutely nothing he could do now to stop himself. He felt his lips part of their own volition, compelling him forwards to meet with Josh's, the soft perfume of his hot breath filling his nose and his mouth, the gentle pressure of those wonderful lips against his, opening them further, until he could resist no longer and pushed back. For those few seconds, everything else in the world melted away and they were all that there was.
"That was the best kiss I've ever had," George murmured.
"That was the only kiss I've ever had," Josh said.

*

George rolled onto his side, keeping his palm under his cheek to protect it from the chilly concrete. With his free hand, he reached out and patted the slope, until he found Josh's hand. George shivered.
Josh moved closer. "It's cold here, isn't it?"
George laughed. "A bit, yeah." Josh moved closer still. "I'm sure there are better places we could have spent our first anniversary."
"Warmer ones, certainly." Josh was shivering too.

George put his arms around him and hugged him tightly. Josh snuggled against him and kissed his cheek. For several minutes, they stayed as they were, listening to the calls of migrating geese flying overhead, the occasional rumble of passing cars. No swans, no boats, just one man and his dog passed them by...

"Padlocks," Josh said.

"Pardon?"

"Why we're here."

"Padlocks," George repeated, frowning for a moment, but then it dawned on him what Josh was talking about. "You locked our love here?"

Josh nodded.

"Where?"

"I'll show you." Josh rolled onto his front and crawled up the slope. George climbed up beside him. "Give me your hand."

George did so and allowed Josh to guide him. His fingers touched cold metal—a short chain. He lifted it over the ledge and blinked in astonishment. "That's my bike lock."

"*Our* bike lock."

"OK, *our* bike lock. And the other one?"

"The lock from my ottoman."

"Ah! I always wondered about that."

"It was symbolic," Josh admitted. "When I came here the first time, I was trying to lock away my feelings. The second time I was setting them free."

George flipped the locks over and saw their initials were engraved into the backs of both. "You did this after the sixth-form ball?"

"Yes."

"It could all have been so different."

"We wouldn't have made it, George. Not without... being apart."

Once again, George pushed aside his regret; he knew Josh was right. What Josh had been through at university would have happened whether they were apart or together, and if they had been together, then Josh would never have met Sean. If Josh had never met Sean…this moment would not have been.

"In my old sketchbook, there are two drawings of this place. One with two bikes, chained together."

"You locked our love here too."

"Yeah." George rolled onto his back and lifted the chain so that the locks dangled above him.

"And the other?" Josh asked.

"The other?"

"You said there were two drawings."

"Oh, err…" George coughed self-consciously.

Josh peered down at him and grinned. "What's the matter with your face? You've gone really pink."

"Sunburn?" George suggested, and they both laughed. "It involves lollipops," he confessed.

"I see. That's interesting." Josh reached inside his coat and then held up his hand. "Show me."

George looked up at the two lollipops, and then at Josh.

"Unless it's likely to get us arrested," Josh qualified.

"Under a viaduct? Do you honestly think—"

"*Show me.*" Josh pushed one of the lollipops between George's lips and popped the other into his own mouth. He settled on his back with his hands behind his head, rolling the lollipop from side to side, sucking and swallowing the sugary saliva created by the motion. In his peripheral vision, he could see George watching him, transfixed, no movement beyond blinking his eyes against the chilly autumn wind whipping under the viaduct. They wouldn't be able to withstand it much longer. Josh pushed the lollipop into his cheek. "So what n—"

Suddenly, the sweet was plucked from his mouth, and George's lips were on his.

Had they still been twelve and thirteen years old, the resultant kiss would have been clumsy and hard-lipped. Instead, it was gentle yet passionate, hot yet sweet. George circled Josh's lips with his tongue.

"You taste…"

"Like Swizzels?" Josh suggested.

"Like you," George said. "And Swizzels."

Josh smiled and kissed George back. "So do you."

They returned to sucking their lollies, or crunching them, in fact. It was too cold not to. When they were done, George looked at the locks again. "What are we doing with these? Putting them back?"

Josh nodded. "No-one's discovered them yet."

"That's because no-one else is crazy enough to turn a concrete viaduct into a love lock bridge," George teased. He put the chain back on top of the ledge and pulled Josh to him once more. "I love you."

"Even though I'm strange?"

"Because you are strange."

Josh frowned and then shrugged. "And I love you." No need to qualify.

With the padlocks safely concealed once more, Josh and George shuffled on their bottoms, down the slope. When they reached the canal bank, Josh rooted in his pocket, trying to locate the keys, but his hands were too cold. He lifted his arms and looked to George for assistance.

"What do you need?"

"The keys. They're in my right pocket."

George put his hands in both pockets and gave Josh a cheeky grin. "Why?"

"We throw them in the canal so nothing can ever come between us."

"We might get new bikes."

"Then we'll get a new lock."

George found the keys and held them out to Josh, but Josh didn't take them. Instead, he hooked their little fingers together. George studied them for a moment.

"I said we'd still be best friends even if I got a boyfriend, didn't I?"

Josh laughed. "Yes. You did."

Together, they lifted their hands over the dark, still water and released the keys. Light surface ripples momentarily distorted the viaduct's reflection, and then it returned to how it had always been; how it would always be.

Acknowledgements

Thanks to Thomas at 2ndcupoftea.com,
for going the extra mile and making enquiries on my behalf.
Your help is very much appreciated.

Über-thanks to the Beaten Track 'crew'.
You are more than authors, editors and proofreaders.
You are wonderful friends and workers of magic.
You make all things possible.

About the Author

Debbie McGowan is an author and publisher based in a semi-rural corner of Lancashire, England. She writes character-driven, realist fiction, celebrating life, love and relationships. A working-class girl, she 'ran away' to London at seventeen, was homeless, unemployed and then homeless again, interspersed with animal rights activism (all legal, honest ;)) and volunteer work as a mental health advocate. At twenty-five, she went back to college to study social science—tough with two toddlers, but they had a 'stay at home' dad, so it worked itself out. These days, the toddlers are young women (much to their chagrin) and Debbie teaches undergraduate students, writes novels and runs an independent publishing company, occasionally grabbing an hour's sleep where she can.

Social Media Links

Website: debbiemcgowan.co.uk and hidingbehindthecouch.com
Newsletter Signup: eepurl.com/b8emHL
Blog: deb248211.blogspot.com
Facebook: facebook.com/DebbieMcGowanAuthor and facebook.com/beatentrackpublishing
Twitter: @writerdebmcg
YouTube: youtube.com/deb248211
Instagram: instagram/writerdebmcg
Tumblr: writerdebmcg.tumblr.com
LinkedIn: uk.linkedin.com/in/writerdebmcg
Goodreads: goodreads.com/DebbieMcGowan
Books2Read: https://books2read.com/DebbieMcGowan

By the Author

I'm not a single-genre author, for which I make no apology. Nor do I write stories of a specific length; I believe a story should be as long as it needs to be.

Thus, to assist you in navigating my catalogue, I've also included the closest-fitting genres and types of publication.

Hiding Behind The Couch Series
(Contemporary/Literary Fiction)

The ongoing story of 'The Circle'...
Nine friends from high school;
Nine friends for life.

The Story So Far...
(in chronological order)

- *Beginnings* (Novella)
- *Ruminations* (Novel)
- *Class-A* (Short Story – also in *Take a Chance* anthology)
- *Hiding Behind The Couch* (Season One)
- *No Time Like The Present* (Season Two)
- *The Harder They Fall* (Season Three)
- *Crying in the Rain* (Novel)
- *First Christmas* (Novella)
- *In The Stars Part I: Capricorn–Gemini* (Season Four)
- *Breaking Waves* (Novella)
- **Chain of Secrets (Novella – also in Love Unlocked anthology)**
- *In The Stars Part II: Cancer–Sagittarius* (Season Five)
- *A Midnight Clear* (Novella – also in *Boughs of Evergreen* anthology)

- *Red Hot Christmas* (Novella)
- *Two By Two* (Season Six)
- *Hiding Out* (Novella – CHO Crossover)
- *Those Jeffries Boys* (Novel)
- *The WAG and The Scoundrel* (Gray Fisher #1)
- *Perfect Tenor* (Novella)
- *The Lost Mitten* (see 'Children's Stories')
- *Reunions* (Season Seven)
- *Tabula Rasa* (Gray Fisher #2)
- *Breakfast at Cordelia's Aquarium* (Short Story)
- *Reverberations* (Novel)
- *To Be Sure* (Novella – also in *Never Too Late* anthology)
- *What A Scorcher!* (Flash Fiction)
- *Goth of Christmas Past* (Front of House #1)
- *The Advent of Reason* (Novella)
- *Not My Christmas* (Novella)
- *Highlights* ~ co-written with A.M. Leibowitz (Short Story – Notes from Boston meets Hiding Behind The Couch)
- *Distractions* (Gray Fisher #3)

Checking Him Out Series
(M/M and LGBTQ Romance)

- *Checking Him Out* (Book One)
- *Checking Him Out For the Holidays* (Novella)
- *Hiding Out* (Novella – Noah and Matty – HBTC Crossover)
- *Taking Him On* (Book Two – Noah and Matty)
- *Checking In* (Book Three)
- *The Making of Us* (Book Four – Jesse and Leigh)

Seeds of Tyrone Series
(M/M Romance)
~ co-written with Raine O'Tierney

- *Leaving Flowers* (Book One)
- *Where the Grass is Greener* (Book Two)
- *Christmas Craic and Mistletoe* (Book Three)

Stand-Alone Stories

- *Champagne* (LGBTQ Historical Novel)
- 'Time to Go' (Contemporary Short in *Story Salon Big Book of Stories*)
- *And The Walls Came Tumbling Down* (Sci-fi Novel)
- *No Dice* (Sci-fi Novel)
- *Double Six* (Sci-fi Novel)
- *Sugar and Sawdust* (M/M Romance Short Story)
- *Cherry Pop Valentine* (M/M Romance Short Story)
- *Coming Up* ~ co-written with Al Stewart (LGBTQ Short Story)
- *Of the Bauble* (LGBTQ Fantasy Romance Novella)
- *So Long, Little Black Diamonds* (True Short Story)
- *The Pastor's Last Drop* (Ongoing Historical Novel – Wattpad)
- *When Skies Have Fallen* (LGBTQ Historical Romance Novel)
- *A Snowy Ball* (When Skies Have Fallen Novelette)
- *The Great Village Bun Fight* (LGBTQ Comedy Novella – also in *Seasons of Love* anthology)
- 'Oh No She Didn't!' (LGBTQ Short Story in *Upstaged!: an anthology of women who love women in the performing arts*)
- *The Great Pretendo* (Flash Fiction)
- 'Nina, Pretty Ballerina' (Short Story in *Play On...: a collection of short stories, poetry and prose, inspired by the songs of ABBA*)
- *Meredith's Dagger* (Contemporary/Historical Feminist/LGBTQ Novel)

Audiobooks

- *And The Walls Came Tumbling Down* – Narrated by Hannibal Mills
- *Checking Him Out* – Narrated by Tim Larkfield
- *Of The Bauble* – Narrated by Jack Hardman
- *The Great Village Bun Fight* – Narrated by Jack Hardman
- *When Skies Have Fallen* – Narrated by Tim Holbourne

Children's Stories (written as J.S. Morley)

- *The Lost Mitten* ~ illustrated by Sofia Oxelstrand
- *Chompy the Velociraptor* ~ illustrated by Kate Andrew
- *Zoom the Pterodactyl*

Beaten Track Publishing

For more titles from Beaten Track Publishing,
please visit our website:

https://www.beatentrackpublishing.com

Thanks for reading!